VANESSA FRANCES

Through Neighboring Windows

Also by Vanessa Frances

laundry
sentiments of youth
in pursuit of kinder muses

*To my friends, my family, my neighbors, and your neighbors—
Let us champion a collective tomorrow.*

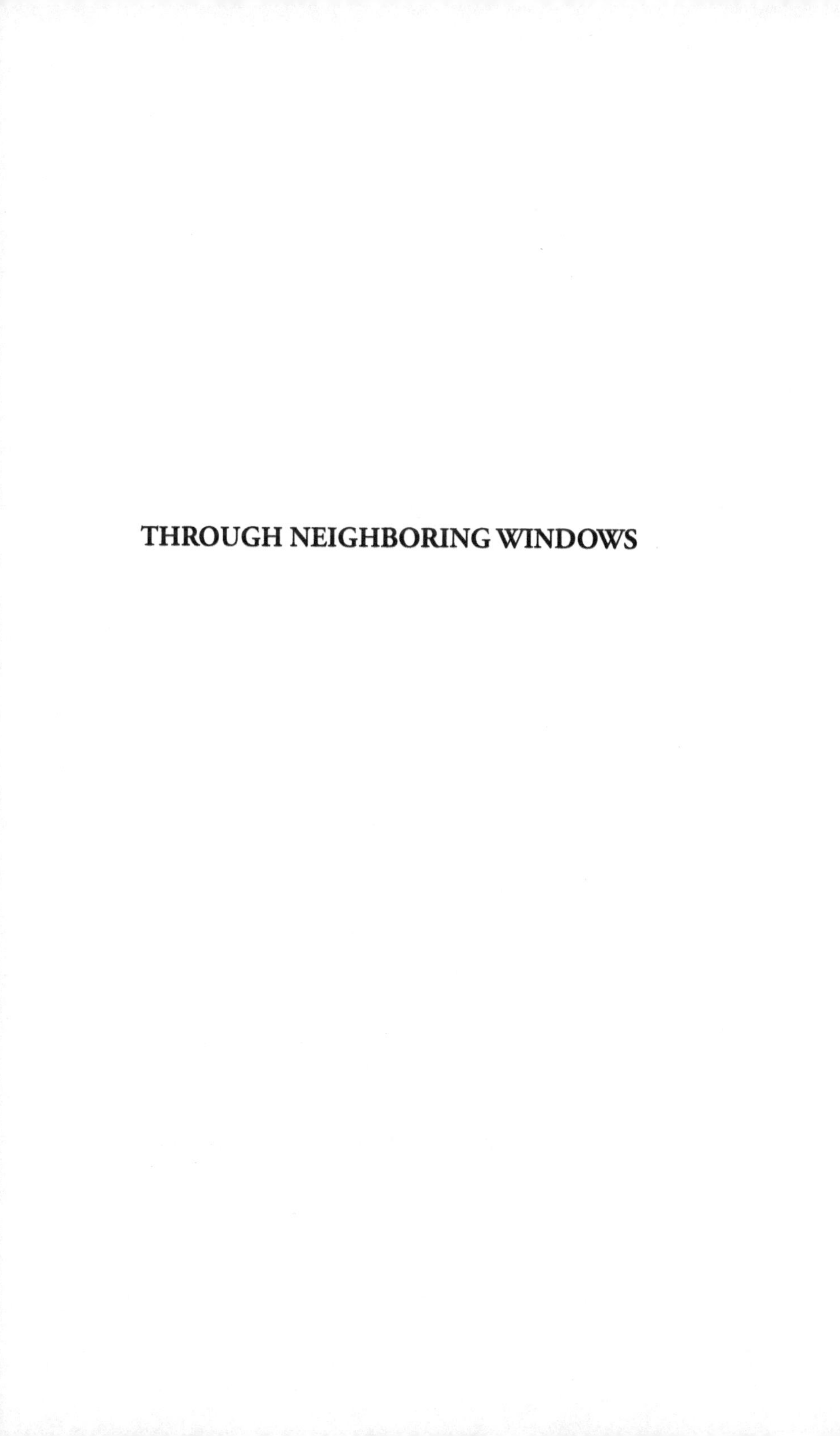

THROUGH NEIGHBORING WINDOWS

Table of Contents

GATES

The old man in the downtown gas station had a Rorschach test on his teeth.

Painted in shadows and flurries, the white space and the hollow bone depicted a tiger halfway into a backbend, poised for cautious rest, or a hunched old woman reaching out clawed fingers. Creatures dove into each other's abdomens with bent arms and narrating fingers, constricting across the spirits of their neighbors.

As the old man spoke, the shapes transformed and distorted themselves in various diagrams and depictions, each becoming less like the last, nonetheless familiar.

The man's lips were pruned and dry, framed around the portrait stained across the bone of his teeth. Expression pained; he had been here a long time, his history printed into his body forever. A part of the attraction. A piece of the property. A relic of existence across once white enamel.

The shadows within his mouth collapsed as the man requested menthols from behind the counter with a stiff motion of his fingers. The cashier obliged, reached up to the shelf, and slid the package across the counter.

The man pulled discolored cash from his tattered pocket, the bills made dark by dirty hands. Lincoln's vacant eyes were blacked out by ash and ink; the crumpled bill smoothed out only when it reached the counter, held up to the cool fluorescent light.

"And a scratcher too," the man cracked his knuckles along the smooth counter edge. "I'm feeling lucky today."

The man mentioned he used to work in construction and built nearly all the homes around here, creating the familiar streets and playgrounds the neighborhood kids had roamed for decades.

"Forty-six and a half years doing that," he mumbled under his breath.

He called himself the Urban Architect, playing god within the city limits. He created structures and buildings for different uses, modeling each project after things he'd seen hitchhiking across the country.

The man modeled his designs after nature, as if imitating it. Bridges he'd crafted were sturdy as stone arches, roads cut like ancient riverways, dug into the ground the way moles stretched canyons and communities of their own into the Earth. Human construction had the same principle, expanding the amount of livable space, but pooling hands and paws extended our reach above the Earth instead of deeper into it.

He'd left when the money dried up, and the billionaires wandered elsewhere for armchair architects without half the knowledge he had of building anything. He said modern houses became less practical, less inspired by the land, and less attractive to him, who'd rather make an intimate library than a modern, stark white house in an open field.

"That's the thing," the man told me, tucking the scratcher between his index and middle finger. "You can be as impractical as you want, as long as you're thinking the way they think. Like God. Untouchable, even in a glass palace."

He spits into his palm and rubs his hands together before holding still, ushering a silent prayer. "If I win this damn thing, I'm building the best house for my wife and kids, better than any shit you've seen before. Something *really* fit for a God."

I imagined the man building a palace with an arm reaching to the stratosphere, competing with the planes for how high it could reach. Maybe he'd place himself at the top, categorizing the storybook stills of other people's lives in timestamps on his hand as he watched them bustle by from above.

The man flicked the ash off his lit cigarette and reached down the sidewalk to jut his pinky into it, smudging out the blueprint of a structure across the sidewalk.

"Five bedrooms, three bathrooms. Hell, maybe a pool. By the beach or up near the hills so that we can see across the city. No more living below the smog lines. God's not living down here; why should I?"

I was surprised by his modesty.

The man had allotted no room in the house for particular excess. Everything was budgeted for comfort, nothing more. As he drew, his fingers stained dark from cigarette ash; I noticed there was no purse closet, no staff house, no twin infinity pools, or bathrooms with smooth marble bordered with gold around the edges.

Maybe this *was* enough for a God.

It wasn't until my older years I realized that most of us do not dream of excess, only of comfort. Excess is taught, a treaty signed in blood and carried like a pair of gold handcuffs. Excess is dropped upon the top of the hierarchy of needs, an ankle weight disguised as a glass house or second jet. Skew the idea enough, and excess could be perceived as comfort. A basic need.

"You don't see animals hoarding all their fucking food, do you?" The man coughed, painting scattered trees outside the house on the sidewalk. "The Greeks knew that the gods were the ones doing any of that shit."

I stood quietly as the man reached into his other pocket and pulled out a quarter, resting the scratcher on the house's roof. Taking a deep breath and scratching across each of the numbers, his eyes flickered back and forth between the winning numbers and his own. He swallowed, reaching the end of the scratcher, and used his stained fingers to clean off the rest of the scratcher.

"It's a dud," the man shrugged, folding up the scratcher and putting it into his pocket. "Least I know the winning numbers next time."

I was about to interrupt, correct him on how the lottery worked, but he was already taking out another cigarette, looking into the parking lot and the racing cars across the main road.

"Salmon," he whispered, fumbling around in his pocket before revealing a dark green lighter. He pointed it across the freeway. "Cars move just like the salmon."

The man tried to hand me a cigarette, which I declined, my eyes still fixated on the roadway, cars jetting between lanes. I imagined many of them were returning from where they came.

There was a bag of gummy worms peeking out of the top of the man's bag. He caught me eyeing them and slid the bag across the sidewalk, smudging his ash-painted blueprint into an indistinguishable discoloration on the ground.

I popped a gummy worm in my mouth, feeling the sticky sweetness pull on the bottoms of my teeth before I swallowed the worm.

"They're pretty good, right?"

The man grinned, and the tiger emerged from his mouth, making space below the man's gums. There was a new figure too, dark and indistinct, a hand outstretched towards the retreating tiger, into the back of the man's mouth and down his throat.

"Can you hand me one?" the man asked, pointing ash-stained fingers towards the bag in my hands. He closed his mouth, encasing the scene before I could get another look.

"Red or blue?"

OUTSIDE

Kat woke to the power outage long before Tony had even stirred.

The room was hot and ripe, hazy with humidity that Kat could feel pressing on the top of her chest. Maybe she was just getting older. Perhaps it was the exhaustion. But if she closed her eyes, it felt like a pair of hands wrapped around her neck, every breath of dense air closing it tighter.

The visual alarmed Kat enough to roll over onto her back, staring straight up at their speckled ceiling and trying to breathe easily. There was no way to go back to sleep.

Trapped under the heat of their ancient comforter, Kat thrust her foot out in search of remaining cold air, only to find none left. Her foot hung limply off the side of the bed, defeated. She huffed.

With the power outage, the streetlights had turned off, making the heat even eerier. The unknowing blurred the separation between inside and out.

It's like sinking into a swamp, Kat thought, *though this would be normal if we weren't people.*

This would just be what living felt like.

She thought of the animals in their habitats, birds in the trees, frogs in the swampy waterway just beyond their house, the raccoons that shuffled through the yard near dusk. There was no distinction between *where* they lived and what they lived *in*, and no place to duck out of the way of nature.

Kat frowned at the thought, preferring the outside not to feel like it was also within. She liked her space, the comfort of separation between herself and the outdoors with everything else that wasn't part of her and Tony's shared bubble.

Though they'd lived in this house for the last few years, it looked different in darkness like this: oddly unfamiliar without the buzzing of their AC or the steady hum of the refrigerator.

Losing that touch of civilization, as small as it seemed, mattered. It made a difference to know that there was a system, a fail-safe to fall back on. Not just the unknown.

This was the third rolling blackout of the summer, and each one had lasted slightly longer than the last, all pushing the nights out longer under the weight of a warming room. Kat sensed with how often they were becoming; it wouldn't be the last, the periods of darkness growing more frequent with the rising price of energy and the instability of the infrastructure.

She thought about the older man that lived down the street alone, hoping he was alright. Kat hoped everyone was alright, really. They all were easing into some tremendous unknown version of reality none of them could have predicted, but here they were.

Her arms prickled with the sweat rising from her armpits. She was surprised she'd slept this long in the heat. Maybe this is what it felt like to get used to it. Even in the darkness of the night, the humidity from the outside began curling its fingers through the walls. Their separation from nature continued to dwindle.

Kat reached up and felt her neck, grazing the tops of her fingers over her skin to feel her sweat.

As Kat sat up, the hot air stuck to her unwashed face.

"Powers out," she grimaced, pushing Tony on the arm until he began to stir. He made several popping noises from his mouth, his jaw cracking before he relaxed again. Grinning, Kat shoved Tony's back, her fingers pulling back the moisture on his skin. Even he was sweating.

"Tony," Kat whispered. "Wake up."

Tony took a deep breath, slowly blinking open his eyes. Sitting up, he frowned, soft age lines forming delicate parenthesis around the outside of his mouth. Kat realized how much older he was beginning to look these days, time carving out new details across his face.

"Fuck…Again?"

"I know. I just want one night without feeling like I'm drowning in our bedroom. This is getting excessive."

Tony scooted the sheets off his bare chest, groaning as he reached for the flashlight on his nightstand. His hand shuffled through papers and the stack of books piled on the small table, grappling until his fingers found the power button. The room flooded with light. Kat squinted and looked around at their room and towards their shadowed street.

Tony frowned.

"What should we do?"

Kat laughed, "Call the power company again? Wait it out? I don't see what our other options are."

Tony set the flashlight down in the center of the bed, casting the light up toward the ceiling. Both forms were faintly visible from the bed in cast shadows against the otherwise dark wall.

"Do you want to take a shower?" Tony asked.

"Together?" Kat replied.

Tony nodded. "Why not?"

Kat reached up, blotting her nose. Her fingers returned slick with oil. She felt sticky and unclean, the sheets unwashed after one too many nights spent in their personal sauna. The power and the water had also been infrequent the past few weeks. Running a load of laundry had felt like an uphill battle, leaving the pair in damp sheets that had begun crossing the line of what was tolerable to sleep under.

Still, Kat was surprised. Tony never asked to shower together anymore, at least, nowhere near as often as they used to.

They fell in love as twenty-somethings. The start of their romance could be painted in scenes of hurried sex between college classes or hidden in the washrooms of the campus gym. Kat vividly remembered kicking Tony out through her single-window college apartment, climbing down before her roommate returned from class.

She'd watched Tony scale down the outside wall to the ground, once landing thigh-deep in a pile of snow. He'd waved at her as he ran up the road back to his dorm, his green coat bouncing through the quiet falling of early morning snow.

In the summer, they'd spent countless afternoons laying on the cool sea green tile of Kat's apartment, wading in their sweat; every bead on their bodies a champion of their labor, hands wandering back towards each other to start over again.

Sweat was different now, water was three times as expensive, and they were old. Not *particularly old*, but old enough to reconsider the cost of giving in to impulse. Youth felt like a mile marker in a mirror; they were lucky now to make love every few months and luckier still when the AC stayed on while they did.

There needed to be more urgency to explore and be with each other now, with fewer new facets and features to experience. Kat and Tony were as close with each other as themselves, the curves of each other's backs, the moles concealed only by undergarments. The rush of novelty had been replaced with a knowing you have when you love someone for long enough, and though it was warm and its own victory, it was different.

"Sure," she replied, feeling adventurous but also filthy. A shower was just one of the many things she wanted, another being a working washing machine.

In the heat of the bedroom, the thought of cold water

pouring down her face and chest sounded more euphoric than any sex she'd ever had.

Tony grinned and pulled the blanket off them both, though the room had grown hot enough that even this offered no relief. The pair followed the thin light of the flashlight down the hallway to the bathroom. Sounds of traffic hummed from the road; people were still stuck in hour-long commutes back to the suburbs from the flashiness of the city, even this late at night.

The singing of crickets from the backyard echoed without the rumbling of the AC to drown them out.

It felt wild inside their small habitat, the last layer of separation gradually becoming thinner and thinner as the heat intensified.

Pushing open the bathroom door, Tony set the flashlight on the counter. The light caught on the twin mirrors above the sink and illuminated the pair just enough to see the outlines of their figures in shadows against the wall.

Though mostly obscured by the limited light, Kat blushed and sheepishly pulled off her pajamas while Tony did the same.

Though hesitant, as if all of this was happening for the first time, both looked over their partner, examining their outlines. They had softened and expanded, new spots sunken in with age and wear, deflating molds of who they used to be.

Kat studied Tony's face as he took the bathmat down. She couldn't remember the last time they were naked together, two animals unbuttoned in a den, without rushing to work or outings with friends, family, or to a crying baby across the hall.

Twirling her wedding band around her finger, Kat caught it in an unfamiliar, new fold of skin. Tony's hair was thinning, patchy at best around the sides of his ears. Spider veins were running up the back of Kat's legs, and Tony desperately needed to shave.

From half-lit mirror reflections, they looked like two well-loved toys, raggedly worn around the edges.

Squinting through the dark, Kat could picture Tony's full head of hair he'd had when they met, always matted but one of her favorite things about him. She'd run her hands through the tangles, challenging herself to bring them to order, though she never did. When she'd tried, within her recent memory, Tony's hair was thin enough not to tangle anymore.

Kat recalled the pair in a house party bathroom decades ago, the door locked with outsiders shaking the handle to try and relieve themselves. They'd been in there for at least half an hour, ignoring the frantic knocking or disgruntled shaking of the brass doorknob as they kissed, talked, and took space from the outside noise.

Kat's eyes had scrambled between Tony's lips and the banging on the door, trying to write her panic out of the moment.

"One second," Tony called, checking the lock.

"Hurry up!" The voice outside replied, banging louder.

Kat's eyes widened. Tony smiled at her, placing a reassuring hand on her shoulder.

Watch this, he mouthed, clearing his throat and lifting his chest as if preparing to walk out on a stage. Kat bit down hard on her lip, holding her hands tightly together.

"Sorry, feeling *really* sick!" Tony released a convincing hurl, covering Kat's mouth to muffle her laugh.

"What?" the voice outside shouted.

"Really-" Tony pretended to hurl again, giving a good gag for an extra measure. Kat brings her hand to her face, closing her smiling eyes.

"-sick," Tony gave a very convincing cough as Kat struggled further to contain her laughter.

Tony grinned and ran his thumb along the outside of Kat's lips, taking off part of her lipstick and staining it along her cheek. She felt it against her skin but didn't move to fix it. It was a mark of their shared existence in that room, of this singular moment.

The two had listened to the footsteps shuffling back and away from the door, breathing a satisfied sigh of relief, followed by frantic hushed laughter.

Tony gently grabbed Kat's hands, pulling her towards the

shower. He bent down, turned on the water, and adjusted the shower head so that the pressure was most intense, the noise overwhelming the rest of the party outside. They were immersed in their private world, and Kat watched patiently. The room filled with steam, warm water casting droplets out and across the bridge of Kat's nose from behind the curtain.

"Do you want to get in?" Tony asked her.

Looking back between the water and the doorknob, Kat nods, pulling Tony in to kiss her. It was warm and wet in their insulated habitat, their singular world. Kat caught a glimpse of the door knob shaking, another frantic entry attempt, but the noise was lost underneath the water and on both occupants. This was just for the two of them.

Now, they stood in the present, bare in the bathroom, hot and uncomfortable in their quiet home. There was no party, noise, or rush to get out of anyone's way. The space of their own that was once just a bathroom wide had nearly tripled, but they'd grown old enough to hardly use it the way they once imagined they would.

It was different now. The people they were back then were nothing more than memory passing through Kat's mind. A relic of another age, their younger selves artifacts of a different era.

But now, nature was rattling the doorknob, and with every passing moment of growing heat, she came closer to opening the door. Their space was threatened, the moment at risk of being completely taken away.

A familiar feeling of nervousness rose in Kat's stomach, and for the first time in decades, she realized there *was* an urgency. A different one, not the same as a drunken party-goer trying to use the bathroom or an anxious authoritarian roommate, but an urgency all the same.

Kat studied the depth between Tony's shoulder and collarbone, reaching out to place her two fingers in the concave, running them up towards his face.

His skin was soft and familiar against her fingers, like a well-made sweater that would always fit.

"You okay?" Tony asked her, reaching down and squeezing the top of her hip. His fingers left a private indentation just above the bone, a print in the living sand of her body.

Shared existence.

Kat leaned forward, placing her hand on the back of Tony's smooth head, the illusion of his old hair dismissed by the absence of a matted sensation of tangled knots. She scratched the bald spot, the thinning parts of his hair, realizing she'd forgotten what the top of his head felt like. It was different having it bare and accessible. Something new.

It felt good. It felt honest.

Getting closer, Kat kissed Tony, disregarding how sweaty they'd both become in their habitat, tasting the salt that had beaded down to his top lip. Crickets and traffic had disappeared underneath the sound of the shower water, and at last, they were utterly alone once again.

Pulling his head back, Tony grinned, lifting his hand to rest just around the outside of her lips. Kat traced the parentheses on the outside of Tony's mouth.

"Do you want to get in?"

Kat smiled and curled her lips together to savor the taste of sweat for a moment longer.

"Yes."

SUPPLICIA CANUM

Of all the dogs Anita walked, Pastor Jacobs' were the absolute worst.

Anita knew she wasn't being biased, or at least, she convinced herself that she couldn't be. In her head after each walk, she tried to give a fair analysis of how the dogs behaved, how they'd dealt with the neighborhood squirrels, and how many times they'd gone to the bathroom.

Anita did this to accurately provide each owner with adequate feedback or offer helpful suggestions for tentative training techniques. She also gave a detailed report on the walk in a short text message write-up she'd send them in the aftermath.

With most of the dogs she walked, owners were responsive to the feedback, making each walk easier than the last.

However, with Pastor Jacobs' dogs, it was increasingly difficult for Anita to think of nice things to say when sending the walk report. After four months of walking Mallory and Marjory, Anita was at her wit's end.

Sitting in her car outside the pastor's house, the cool air conditioner prickled the tips of Anita's fingers. She'd scavenged her brain for parts of the walk that weren't as bad as the bulk of it had been. Sweat soaked through the arms of her t-shirt, half attributed to the heat, half the amount of cortisol in her bloodstream.

Mallory kept a consistent pace on the walk. Marjory only chased one squirrel. No one ate any poop. No neighbors were harmed.

Anita looked out into the wealthy neighborhood that the Jacobs family lived in, tall fences, a gate requiring a combination, broad front porches, and tailored flower beds. She always felt disoriented in these neighborhoods, as if the deep desire for something familiar and friendly had morphed so far that it turned the community into something that couldn't be lived in, like a movie set or a generic painting from Walmart.

Great!

Pastor Jacobs and his wife Marylin would reply in their group chat, followed by several thumbs-up emojis, the two of them completely unaware of how challenging the walk had *really* been.

Mallory had knocked Marjory to the ground while wrestling over who could chase a dog and his owner jogging on the opposite sidewalk. Anita fell to the ground, scuffing up her knees, and landed in Mallory's shit. Marjory had licked it off Anita's knees, so she realized part of that last walk report entry had been a bit of a lie, but she was so fed up and exhausted that she didn't care, even if it meant lying to a pastor.

Does that send me to a specific circle of hell? Anita wondered, racking her brain for any references to punishment over lying to a pastor regarding lying about a dog eating shit within *The*

Divine Comedy but returning with none.

Anita wanted so badly to quit working for the pastor; it wasn't like the money was that good: $15 a walk, only twice a week. She could earn that easily with other clients or at her old job at the downtown clothing store with her friends Lea and Natalia, and that didn't require walking two sled dogs in training that didn't obey basic commands.

Anita daydreamed about walking more patient boxers or tiny Yorkies, dogs with even temperament, quiet in the face of new variables, and attentive when she shouted, *"No!"*

Still, Anita was back at the Jacobs' residence that Tuesday afternoon, scavenging for the spare key hidden inside the faux sprinkler in their front yard. She thumbed the key between her thumb and pointer finger, apprehensive as she walked to the front door. She could feel the hesitation – no, strike that – the *agony*, all the way through her bones the closer she got to the front.

Why do I keep saying yes? She wondered. *I'd rather get my flu shot for a second time and maybe even a third. Or sit in line without an appointment at the DMV.*

Or –

She hesitated on the thought but determined that she really did mean it-

Lick the floor of Melbas downtown. Yup. I'd rather lick the floor of the worst dive bar in town than do this again.

Anita huffed, looking down at the key in her hands. She could hear Mallory and Marjory whimpering on the other side of the glass door, hot breath leaving storm clouds on the bottom panel that concealed their panting pink tongues on the other side.

Taking a deep breath, steadying herself, and lowering her expectations entirely, she pushed the door open.

Both dogs jumped at her immediately. Anita put her hands behind her back and pushed past the two of them, searching for their leashes and trying to avoid any more scratch marks on her legs.

"Hi, *yes*, I see you," Anita whispered over the dog's urgent whelping. "It's okay. I'm here. We're gonna walk in one second."

The request for patience didn't resonate with Mallory or Marjory. Both dogs barked louder as Anita rushed to the kitchen to find the leashes neatly folded on the counter beside the treats they were to be given after the walk (even if Anita didn't think they deserved it, which, in her objective opinion, they never did).

A framed photo of the Jacobs family stared Anita down as she clipped the dogs into their harnesses. The portrait had been professionally painted, with eerie amounts of detail. It looked almost as if the Jacobs were a royal family from the 1600s the way they were stylized: high foreheads and narrow eyes, stoic expressions unsmiling, even their younger children and beautiful teenage daughter looked haunting.

Anita hated the painting, the way the eyes followed her around the room every time she came over to walk the dogs, as if the whole family knew she was lying to them about how poorly Mallory and Marjory behaved. She shuddered at the thought.

The family portrait was surrounded by a golden frame that hung against a museum white wall. Mrs. Jacobs had told Anita they were commissioning some new art. Anita only hoped it was being done in a style much less... *Renaissance.*

The Jacobs' family's whole house was painted in that stark, sterile white, with its tall ceilings and romantic windows. It might as well have been a museum, especially when you considered the painting that neighbored the family portrait was one of Jesus Christ himself, dark eyes looming over the room, straight out of 14th century Italy.

Anita couldn't imagine eating breakfast under the watchful eyes of God every morning, afraid he might judge her for eating her sugar-fruit-based cereal or for reusing a dirty coffee mug before she'd washed it.

Anita didn't have anything against people that practiced a

religion. She actually thought it was pretty admirable to do so. However, she had no desire to invite the presence of something that always cast a cloud of judgment over her into a space as intimate as the kitchen. She could do that enough by herself.

"Let's behave today," Anita whispered, turning the silver door handle and letting the heavy summer air into the too-cold house. *"Please."*

Ignoring her, the dogs were off, pulling Anita down the stairs and across the street. Anita jogged to keep up. She struggled to pull back on their leashes, each dog hurrying in a different direction, stretching her arms far enough that she feared they would snap right off.

"Slow DOWN!" Anita huffed and yanked the leashes back. The dogs gagged, and Anita felt temporarily guilty before they lunged forward again. Mallory and Marjory were undeterred by Anita's brief attempt at discipline, each racing to pee on the spots the other one had already marked, knotting their leashes into a single rope in the race back and forth between the different trees and bushes. Anita pulled the leashes back again, but the dogs persisted, running their Iditarod to the lamppost on the corner.

While the dogs were distracted by the messages in pee left behind by dogs running in past races to the lamppost, Anita hunched over and tried to unwind the two leashes from each other, completely out of breath.

Another day of guessing what I could possibly say to these people, Anita thought. *Maybe I'll mention their... Enthusiasm. Definite enthusiasm.*

Suddenly, a tightening sensation spread across Anita's right hand. Both dogs lurched forward away from the pole just as her fingers reached the center of the knotted leashes, and her fingers caught a gap in the knot before the dogs yanked forward and constricted the leash around Anita's fingers, swelling them red.

"Stop, stop, *STOP!*" Anita shouted, digging her heels in the grass as the dogs began leaping towards the crosswalk and into the truck barreling down the sidestreet. The driver honked, startling the dogs just out of its path. Leaning back with all her weight, Anita pulled the dogs out of the road, but in the process, came tumbling down onto her back, landing on both her elbows. Her fingers, at least, came free.

The dogs panted in familiar patterns, finally still but uninterested in Anita's fall. They both walked in gentle circles around where Anita landed as if idling in place before the walk could continue. Mallory finally sat, leaning her head down to sniff the grass. Marjory stared at Anita, panting in a smile.

Anita got the leashes untangled and then leaned down to inspect her elbow. Before she saw it, warmth spread from the joint to her wrist when she straightened her arm. The heat transformed into a deeper burn, then an ache. When she reached down to touch one of her elbows, her fingertips returned to her stained crimson.

"Fuck."

The dogs stopped panting and tilted their heads. "Sorry, you've probably never heard that before."

Anita took a deep breath and let her eyes take in the rest of the damage. It was somehow worse and better than she thought it would be: Road rash revealed raw red skin, and blood, from her elbow down to just above her wrist. The impact had already left a dark bruise.

Mallory and Marjory bounced their tails in the grass, tongues hanging out of their mouths in adjacent angles, uninterested and unknowing.

Anita gritted her teeth, putting her free hand down to push back to her feet. Her arm stung as if it had been marked with a branding iron as the dogs continued to pant.

"I'm done," Anita finally huffed, yanking both the dogs back in the opposite direction towards the house. "They can find a new dog walker, maybe a bodybuilder, Cesar Millan, or whatever masochist volunteers to do this next. But it's not gonna be me."

Mallory and Marjory dug their feet into the grass and pulled at the end of the leash, desperate to continue the walk. Mallory turned her head, yanking the leash into her mouth as if she and Anita were playing a game of Tug of War, her deep brown muzzle fixed over the leash, shaking her head with every pull.

"We're not *playing*," Anita insisted, "We're going *home!*"

The dogs protested in whimpers, and Mallory returned to pulling on the leash at full force.

"No Mallory!" Anita pulled the leash out of Mallory's mouth, causing her to wince in pain. For the first time, Mallory went silent; ears flipped back against the top of her head, eyes low.

"You need some help?"

Anita saw an older man holding his garden hose to a rosebush in his front yard. His dark sunglasses concealed his eyes, but the man's skin and face were worn from the sun, deep wrinkles covering his hands.

She felt like she'd seen him in the neighborhood before, reading a fanned open newspaper at 11 am on a Tuesday with a hot cup of coffee on his porch, no matter the outdoor temperature. She thought she remembered him saying hello a few times when she'd been out with the dogs. Still, she wasn't sure. Doing this job, she encountered many people in cookie-cutter neighborhoods like this one. After a while, they all started to blur together. Faces were the one thing Anita always struggled to remember.

"I'm fine, thanks," Anita huffed, yanking the dogs forward. They wouldn't budge.

"You're bleeding," the man remarked. "Can I at least get you a bandage?"

"I'm-"

"-fine, sure, but I don't want your blood all over the sidewalk. Brings down the property value. Let me get you a bandage."

Before she could say another word, the man rushed into the house, leaving Anita beside the lamppost with both dogs laying down in the grass.

The heat was worse that day than it had been all summer,

so of course, this was the day the dogs decided to push her to her limit. Anita swore she heard another heat advisory on the radio in the car today. From what she'd logged in her head, it was happening more lately, for at least thirteen days this month. That was a record for the state, but meteorologists were emphasizing it was just a "once in a lifetime" kind of event. Anita thought these "once in a lifetime events" seemed to be ramping up in frequency, diluting the meaning for the general public.

But maybe it felt diluted because Anita remembered *too* many things that most people would label "once in a lifetime." Her dad had died in an airplane crash when she was seven, and her younger sister had battled leukemia for nearly as long as she'd been alive. Anita had escaped a burning building in college, saw her best friend get struck by lightning at a golf course, and watched her grandparent's house in Florida go underwater on the six-o'clock news. Anita had lived through and remembered all of it, the "once in a lifetime" moments stored in a file folder next to all the mundane data her brain could never seem to stop collecting.

Anita thought for a long time she'd use her hyperattentive memory for something like climate law or biology, an industry where she could make a difference and impact people like her dad did as a doctor. She'd always been good with numbers, incredibly detailed, and observant of everything that ever happened.

Still, Anita watched the world collapse while not working in any of the fields, trying to prevent it, and it made her feel sick to her stomach. After twelve years of being a leading student through high school, Anita thought she had burned up all her good juices by the time she was pitter-pattering through a General Studies degree in college. Perpetually exhausted, she clamored to the college finish line, hung up the diploma on the single open wall of her studio apartment, and resigned herself to walking dogs.

A bluejay swept down into the lower branches of the tree

neighboring the lamppost, sending Mallory and Marjory into a suddenly attentive haze, but luckily, not hysteria. Marjory hovered on her belly, preparing to pounce up towards the tree's base, gently yanking on Anita's arm.

"Marjory, stop," Anita says weakly. "I've had enough of this."

The dogs stilled, but their attention didn't waver from the tree.

Climate scientists didn't walk dogs to pay their bills; Anita was sure of it. If she wanted to make a difference so badly, she should've pushed on herself more while in college and connected with people who knew what they were doing because Anita, didn't.

Beyond notating which dogs had gone to the bathroom, taken multiple drinks from the water bowls, chased 'x' number of squirrels, or behaved friendly with others, Anita's good memory and the mark of making an impact was resigned to filling out checkboxes on an app.

"Alright, come here."

The man reappeared on the porch, a bottle of rubbing alcohol and a bandage in his hand. Anita yanked on both the dogs, but still, they would not budge. Seeing her struggling, the man jumped from the porch and approached her instead. He smelled like warm wood and sunscreen, familiar smells that reminded Anita of her father.

"Let me see your arm," he asked her. Anita turned her arm over and let him look at the wound. He breathed in sharply between his teeth.

"You got it good."

"I could feel it," Anita replied, feeling his stern grip on her arm.

"Doesn't seem like anything's broken," he rotated Anita's arm on its side. She winced.

"You'll survive," he laughed. "Sorry about that."

The man dabbed a cotton ball with some of the rubbing

alcohol. "I just washed my hands, promise."

Anita nodded, looking away as he placed the soft cotton on her arm. She bit her bottom lip; the wound stung worse than she thought it might.

"Breathe," the man reminded her. "How do you expect your body to relax if you let your brain tense up like that?"

Dropping her shoulders, Anita took a full breath through her nose, sent it out of her mouth, and then repeated. The stinging gradually became less intense, and the man wrapped a gauze bandage around her arm.

"Only leave this on for a bit," he instructed firmly. "You want the wound to air out, and it'll heal faster if it can breathe."

"Thank you." Anita nodded. "You didn't have to do any of that."

"Like I told you," the man responded, setting the bottle of rubbing alcohol down on the ground. "I didn't want your blood getting all over the sidewalk." He paused, pushing the dark sunglasses up onto the top of his head.

"Robin," he said, reaching his hand out.

"Anita."

"I see you out here every once and a while. Are you the full-time dog walker for the Jacobs?"

Anita nodded, looking back at Mallory and Marjory, who had both gotten cozy again.

She considered telling him that today was the day she'd decided to quit, but decided that he'd probably realize it when she didn't come back. Endings were funny that way, you could choose how much or little you wanted to partake in them, but even then, they still happened.

"They're pretty rough dogs to deal with, huh?"

Anita shook her head quickly, as she had no idea what Robin would report back to the Jacobs, "No, no, they're fine. It was just an accident."

Robin narrowed his eyes. "You don't have to be cordial about it. My wife walked the two of them once and nearly blew out her shoulder."

"Really?"

"Really," Robin replied.

"Has your wife ever walked them again?"

Robin shook his head. "Maria passed away a few years ago."

Anita shook her head. "I'm so sorry."

Robin waved his hand. "You've got nothing to be sorry for."

Anita looked down at the dogs, the burning in her arm gradually subsiding. "They're fine dogs, sweet at times even, just antsy. Honestly, this is as still as I've ever seen them."

She looked at Mallory and Marjory, sitting completely still and relaxed on the grass. Anita thought they might even stay in that same spot even if she dropped their leashes.

"If they're running with that energy, I'm not surprised they tire out so quickly. Between trying to pull you and get to whatever scent they've picked up, you can only drive yourself on a motor for so long," Robin laughs.

Anita nodded, looking up to see a small group of birds circling the top of the neighborhood. They fell in line, swooping together and off in one direction. She liked observing their movement and how coordinated and concise it was.

"Those birds are always hanging around here." Robin followed Anita's gaze. "I swear they're following the college bus route sometimes. I see them when I'm on the porch in the mornings."

Robin tucked the rest of the gauze in his pocket, the two standing in silence outside the panting dogs. Neither dog budged from their spots on the grass, and Anita tilted her head back, staring up at the sky.

This felt hopeless. It was another thing to add to her mounting list of things Anita no longer felt capable of doing. Not only could she not get herself up and running, but she couldn't get dogs to either.

"What do you get up to besides dog walking? Are you still in school?" Robin asked.

Laughing, Anita grappled for the right kind of response. She shook her head and said, "No, I'm just doing this right now."

"Well, what would you *like* to be doing?"

Anita paused. Of course, she'd pondered the question before, where she could be if she just pushed on herself and put herself in the right places instead of settling.

She could be in a big city, arguing on behalf of innovative environmental conservation and preservation policies. She could be in a laboratory, researching forest restoration practices and finding a better way to capture and eliminate carbon. So much more significant work existed beyond walking dogs, but she was afraid that she couldn't do any of it because if she were, wouldn't she have done it by now?

"Something... meaningful, I guess." Anita shrugged. "Something that makes an impact."

Robin looked up at the coordinated birds. "It doesn't have to be anything complicated. For example, I can tell you that an old retired guy like myself enjoys sitting on his porch with his coffee, reading the paper, and occasionally, going for a walk at the park where my wife and I used to go. That brings a lot of meaning to me."

"I guess-" Anita frowned. "I guess I'm looking for something without knowing what I'm looking for."

Robin nodded, looking down towards a now-sleeping Mallory and Marjory. "You know, I've read that the best way to tame an out-of-control dog is to be firm but positive—no extra energy. Dogs will sense that and run with it. They can feel your excessive force, whether it's physical or anxious. It's important to conserve yourself and then extend outwards to guide them."

Anita frowned.

"Try it," said Robin. "Really. My wife was like you; she used too much force and spent too much time bracing instead of guiding her energy to react. Just try it."

Taking a deep breath, Anita turned to the dogs. "Hey," she called, gentle but firm. "Let's go home... Come on, let's go."

Neither dog moved momentarily, both content lying out in the cool grass. Anita took a deep breath and swallowed back her frustration.

No excessive force.

"Come on, girls, let's go home."

Suddenly, Mallory and Marjory stood up, stretching their long legs before trotting over to meet her back on the sidewalk. They looked up at her, no longer panting, just attentive.

"See what I mean?" said Robin. "Sometimes you just gotta get in their flow state. Dogs know when they're ready."

"It sounds like you'd be a really good dog walker," Anita laughed, reaching down and patting Mallory on the head.

Robin shook his head. "I've done enough of that," Robin grinned. "Happy to pass it forward."

Anita heard several birds making excited chirps from the trees, but still, the dogs wouldn't take their attention off her.

"You ready to go home?" Anita said again, encouraged by their responsiveness. Mallory turned, gently leading the pack toward the house, Marjory following closely behind.

"There you go," Robin called after her, grinning. "Go easy! Dogs need that, people, too!"

"Thank you!" Anita called back, "Nice to meet you!"

She shouted as she turned back to see Robin nod, waving her off and taking the rubbing alcohol back inside.

It was a calm walk back to the house, the dogs jumping up to the porch, sitting still while Anita removed their harnesses behind the closed door. She brought everything into the kitchen, both dogs following closely at her heels as she refilled their water bowls.

Eagerly taking a drink, the dogs leaned down and drank as much water as possible before laying back down to rest their bellies against the cool tile.

Anita looked back up at the portrait of Jesus on the wall, his knowing eyes, and his kitchen kingdom. She noticed that the frame was a bit crooked, so standing on her tiptoes, she straightened it out. She stepped back from the wall and observed the painting in its intended position. It looked better like this, making Jesus' eyes less judgemental and more fatherly.

The dogs finished their water and plopped patiently in front of Anita, waiting for their traditional post-walk treat. Anita thumbed them into her hand, tossing one to each dog, patting them on the top of the head, and walking back towards the front door. Her arm didn't even sting anymore.

"Nice job today, girls," Anita called back, stepping outside and locking the door before placing the key back in its hiding spot.

Today, she meant it.

The air was still uncomfortably warm, lingering on the top of her skin like flannel sheets. Her car's AC was a welcome change, and she took out her phone to type today's report for the Jacobs.

All was well, she started typing but then paused, deleting the sentence.

She thought about her dad, which was something she didn't let herself do often. She recalled the age lines around his eyes, the kindness of his grin. How their eyes were almost identical shades of green.

Maybe she was better with faces than she thought.

Robin's cologne, still on her arm where he'd wrapped his hand, filled her nose with the same smell she remembered begging her father to put on her in the morning before he went to work or in the bottle she stole from his medicine cabinet after the funeral.

For the first time in longer than she could remember keeping track of, Anita let herself cry. She let herself feel her dad's absence. She remembered her sister in the hospital. She *had* memorized the details of both of their faces, and she let herself visualize them, sitting with it.

She grieved the version of herself that once gave up.

She let herself feel the loss, the time, the energy, the space, the hurt—all of it.

And then, she let it go.

Wiping her cheek with the back of her hand, fingers hovering over the phone keyboard, Anita visualized the birds soaring overhead and the idea of releasing the leashes.

She looked out her window and spotted the birds soaring over the street in real-time. Anita watched as the frontrunner grew tired and migrated to the back of the formation, remaining in sync.

Anita took a deep breath.

One of our worst walks, Anita typed.

But, with a bit of redirection, it got better. I'll see them tomorrow.

Anita opened her car window and hit send.

ROOTS

Cleo loved her tomato plant.

She stored it on the top shelf of her bathroom, where the humidity was plentiful, and the corners of its leaves could reach up against the glass towards the sunlight. The plant was just two months old but had already given her five plump cherry tomatoes. Each was a delightful deep red, bursting on her teeth and filling her mouth with seeds.

The only thing Cleo liked nearly as much as tomatoes were strawberries. She wasn't sure why; maybe it was something about the color red.

Today was Saturday, and the humidity was overflowing in Cleo's bathroom, filling it with dense heat. Cleo tried taming her unruly hair, picking knots from her matted, graying blonde hair.

She thought it was important to look her best today, smudging brown eyeshadow across her eyelids.

For the first time in a month, Cleo had plans today. She had a date.

The date was tonight at seven, at a restaurant just a few miles from her house. It looked like a nice place, according to the photos she'd pulled up on Google: tall white columns, huge open windows, and wooden floors.

She couldn't believe in all the years she'd lived here that, she'd never seen this place before. Had she known about it, she'd have begged several past suitors to take her through the solid wood doors, showing her off on their arm to the other patrons.

Nevertheless, Cleo was excited.

After reading the menu online, she knew that the restaurant served seafood, and Cleo had written down what she might like to order in a notebook she'd slid into the pale green purse she was planning on wearing tonight. The problem was she didn't have a single dress to match.

Deciding that wouldn't be a problem, Cleo swung open the bathroom door back into her bedroom, nearly tripping on the boxes scattered all over the floor. She'd find a dress made to make the whole restaurant notice.

In her excitement for this evening, Cleo had strewn clothes all around the room, looking for something to match the green purse. The fabric of multiple skirts and dresses clumped into canyons across her bedroom's landscape, casting the tight space in a kaleidoscope of color. Still, none of them fit the image she had in her head of what she wanted to look like tonight.

Marching back through the discarded fabric, Cleo felt her foot brush against something heavy on the floor. Looking down, Cleo discovered she'd knocked over her bookshelf last night in the frenzy. It had gotten lost underneath the eighth wonder of the world she'd carved out of her bedroom, the bottom wooden corner barely visible from underneath an array of fabric.

Carefully, she lifted the heavy bookshelf onto the top of her back, pushing it up against the wall until it was fully upright. Only a few books had been casualties in the frantic search for green fabric, while the rest had managed to hold on to the shelf.

On the floor resides an aged copy of *Galapagos* by Kurt Vonnegut and a new-age book of medicine she'd *borrowed* from a bookstore yesterday were both flipped onto their backs on the floor, *Galapagos* bending at the corner.

Cleo had almost entirely forgotten about that trip to the bookstore, remembering only being there for a moment, then in the next, having arrived back home, the book buried deep in the green purse. She was unsure how she'd gotten the book, but perhaps someone nice had let her keep it. She placed both books back on the top shelf, unaware she'd shoved them in spine-side first.

If there was nothing here for her to wear, she decided she'd better get out and go somewhere that might have something suitable.

Cleo piled her hair on top of her head in a heavy ponytail and gathered what she needed to take to the clothing store to find a dress. After finding her chapstick under a navy blue skirt, her wallet behind a ripped blanket, and her sequined belt, she paced back and forth within the room twice before reaching for the door handle.

Before she stepped out into the hallway, she looked behind her towards the bathroom, where the tomato plant sat in the bathroom window, its small green leaves lifted as if waving her goodbye.

"Oh alright," she sighed, stepping back into the bathroom and picking the tomato plant up by the pot. "I guess you can come with me."

Cleo couldn't remember the last time she'd driven anywhere or where her car was, so her journey to the clothing store would be by bicycle.

Carefully, she flung the green purse over her shoulder, making sure it was well out of the way of slipping off her shoulder and getting caught on the bicycle gears, and placed the tomato plant in the cupholder on the handlebars. Cleo twisted the tomato plant into place in the cupholder, making sure it was secure, before pushing up the kickstand and starting down the road.

Cleo wasn't sure why she knew this, but there was a clothing store that wasn't too expensive just around the corner from where she was living.

Since it was a Saturday morning, the roads were quiet, and Cleo biked lazily on the street, listening for cars but hearing none. Though it was warm, there was still an unmistakable breeze, which pulled her hair out from its ponytail and sent it in streamers down her back.

The wind reminded Cleo of the Bahamas, where she'd lived for several years. After becoming discouraged in America, fed up with college and the constant feeling of being rushed everywhere, she decided she'd find somewhere else to call home.

She worked at a snorkeling business on the island of Bimini, convincing the woman that ran it that she could learn quickly. She spent her days swimming, working with tourists, and teaching them how to snorkel using techniques she'd found on Wikipedia. Bimini was famous for a shipwreck off its coast, and Cleo led daily tours to it. Tourists were excited to have someone familiar, an American woman, show them around the Caribbean island. Cleo was not an expert on Bimini or anything related to snorkeling, but she was exceptional at getting tourists to give her money.

She had met several people in Bimini, including the father of her daughter. Living in Bimini felt like a daydream, every part of reality oversaturated with bliss to the point it all felt utterly surreal. No one was breathing down her neck and telling her how to live her life. There was always something new and exciting to do, and nothing felt boring or mundane.

She liked that a lot.

When she'd left Bimini with her daughter, for several reasons she couldn't remember, she'd lost touch with most of her friends and her daughter's father. She wasn't sure where he was now, and for the most part, she wasn't concerned. Although, sometimes, when she'd spent most of the day alone, letting her thoughts wander, she imagined herself still living on the island and raising their daughter by the ocean instead of living alone in the swamp.

Suddenly, a pickup truck sped out of the neighborhood and around the bend of the road, sending Cleo swerving out into the bike lane. The truck roared its engine, racing through the yellow light and ahead on the street, ignoring Cleo completely.

She heard an intense, loud noise in the distance, impossible forces colliding together and echoing throughout the space surrounding it, and she flinched. Cleo looked backward for a moment, hesitating.

Had there been an accident?

She could have broken a bone if she hadn't been paying attention, but luckily, Cleo had survived much worse than that. As for the driver, she didn't know.

Besides, she had a dress to find.

Catching her breath, she reached out, feeling the cupholder, her hands racing along all parts of the tomato plant, looking for bumps and bruises, broken stems, or torn leaves. Luckily, the tomato plant had survived her evasive maneuver. She cupped the base of the plant's stem between her fingers, leaning down and planting a kiss on the side.

"You're safe. Don't you worry."

She kicked back onto the bike, continuing her journey down the sidewalk, this time more cautious.

Shortly after, Cleo reached one of the busiest intersections in their small city and rolled the bike up to a scurried halt beside the pedestrian walk button. The stream of cars was steady here, the faucet of the weekend traffic at full force. The cars moved like fish rushing through a river.

Cleo placed her hand firmly on the handlebars, steadying the tomato plant against the racing wind coming out of traffic as its stem waved back and forth with the passing cars.

The walk sign turned white, and Cleo kicked off her bike and set out through the crosswalk, turning and looking over both of her shoulders repeatedly. She would not be surprised by another car, no way.

The sun was bright, and Cleo could feel her exposed

shoulders prickling in the heat. It was so much warmer than she remembered it being as a child, the weight of the weather making this familiar route seem longer than ever.

Along with the intense heat, the whole city had hit a growth spurt in her absence. When she returned, the buildings were taller, and the once quiet streets had become dense with people. The city was fuller, with new titan skyscrapers and main roads bulldozed through former sidestreets.

There were moments when Cleo felt like a stranger here, most of which she ignored, but sometimes she found herself severed from the reality around her, floating in a place that no longer existed.

One of the nice parts about moving back to your hometown was that there were people that knew you from before you left that had stayed behind. To them, you were still the exciting person that decided to leave in the first place.

Cleo had left town as an adventurer and hero and returned an icon. She'd explored the world and lived somewhere people here had only seen in coffee table books or television documentaries. When she'd run into groups of people, she knew before she'd moved, her time in Bimini could be anything she wanted it to be. She'd been a professional skydiver to some and a bed and breakfast owner to others. To others still, she'd been the wife of a millionaire, responsible for the most extensive housing development in all of Bimini.

However, the lies were much harder to spin when they asked her why she'd left Bimini behind.

"My ex-husband was a *monster*," she'd always tell people, lowering her voice and softening her expression. "It was best I took our daughter away, back to the safety of the States."

Cleo felt better as their faces softened in sympathy with her story, and though she'd made up the details, she was safe in their knowing expressions. They'd take her hand and tell her how brave she was for leaving, even if it broke her heart. They'd remind her that everyone here supported and loved her, no matter what.

People loved feeling like they'd been let in on a secret,

and it didn't matter if it was true or not. It was the feeling of *knowing* that counted, and Cleo knew she could leverage that to her advantage.

Finally across the street, Cleo looked up at the fluorescent sign of the clothing store, an open sign blinking on and off in the window. She parked her bike on the outer part of the sidewalk walkway, looking down at the tomato plant.

"Do you want to stay out here?" she asked, rubbing one of the leaves between her fingertips. She waited gingerly, stroking the top of the stem.

"Oh, alright, I guess you can come in with me. It'll be good to get your opinion."

The store's front door was heavy and jingled as Cleo pried it open. She held the tomato plant in her left hand, running her thumb gently down one of the leaves. The AC from inside brushed the leaf back against her finger, crossing them one over the other.

Many young people were in the store, scattered around the different sections of shirts and pants, everything color coated in streamlined aisles.

Cleo meandered over to the dresses, finding her size and grinning to find how many different shades of green dresses there were. She took the purse off her shoulder and held the bag up to every dress in the section, looking for the perfect match.

"Do you need help finding anything?" A sweet, cheery voice called behind her over the sounds of metal hangers clinking across the racks.

"No, I think I'm just fine, thanks," Cleo answered, her attention drawn back to the hundreds of green dresses, glazing her finger over them as she meandered through the aisle.

"What do you think of this one?" she whispered to the tomato plant. "Surely it's a bit too dark for me."

The tomato plant almost lifted its leaves in a shrug.

"Maybe it's worth trying on."

Cleo pulled the dress off the rack, turning forward to walk down the rest of the aisle.

"Mom?"

This time, the same cheery voice returned in a hurried whisper from over her shoulder. A hand appeared on her wrist, small and slight like her own, pulling on her hand that was wrapped tight around the tomato plant.

"Excuse me, you're going to hurt him," Cleo urged, almost hissing, jerking her hand back from the girl. "Don't you see he's *little?*"

Her hand retreated, and the girl looked back at Cleo with deep amber eyes and tight curls tumbling over her shoulders.

Cleo met the eyes of her near doppelganger's eyes only after recognizing the cool white striped scar on the top of her forearm.

Cleo would know that scar anywhere, no matter what. There was no reframing something that never faded, no hometown reunion for something as permanent as a carving in stone.

There had been a heated exchange between two adults, leaving a baby shoved into the sharp frame of a window. It was a scar Cleo had to explain to teachers, to friends, and to herself, no matter what she did to try and forget. It was an accident, but one she was responsible for.

"Lea?"

Lea frowned, biting down on her lip.

"Mom, what are you doing here?"

"I- I needed a dress. I have a date tonight." Cleo stumbled, feeling flustered, her heart thumping in her chest.

Lea crossed her arms across her chest, eyes flickering between the tomato plant, the green purse, and her mother.

Cleo, suddenly self-conscious, used her free hand to brush some of the dirt off her unwashed pants. She looked smaller, standing next to her daughter, who had her father's tall stature, but Cleo's narrow bones. Lea looked so much older, stone-faced, but her eyes gave away the childlike fear in her expression.

"I asked you not to come to where I work. Do you remember that?" Lea lowered her voice to match her gaze.

"You're going to get me in trouble if you don't leave."

Cleo's hands fumbled around the dress hanger. Is that why she remembered there was a clothing store nearby?

Because Lea worked here?

Or because Lea had told her specifically *not* to come?

Cleo stood back, suddenly offended. "Your boss would just throw out a paying customer?"

"With what *money*?" Lea huffed.

"Mine. My money. You know that. I never said no to you, *never*." The words tumble out of Cleo's mouth, sharp and unfeeling, as her grip tightened around the tomato plant.

Lea took a deep breath.

"Can you *please* leave?"

"No. No, I won't." Cleo pulled the plant close to her body. "I haven't done anything wrong. I'm here to buy a dress."

Lea stepped further into Cleo's row, her hip brushing through all the green dresses until she was inches from Cleo.

"Have you been drinking?" she asked.

Cleo clenched her jaw.

"Lea, you know I haven't had a *single* sip since before I got pregnant."

Lea frowned. "Mom, you promised."

The strength in Lea's expression wavered. "I… I can't stand to see you like this anymore. We talked about this…"

Cleo held tightly to the tomato plant, her grip pushing some of the soil up to the brim of the pot and sprinkling it down onto the carpet. Lea's eyes followed the brown flurries all the way to the floor; lips pressed tightly together.

Lea's eyes flipped to the tomato plant in Cleo's clenched hands and bloodshot eyes. She traced the lines of Cleo's face, her gaze catching the distortion around Cleo's nose, the skin around the outside sagging and inflamed. Cleo looked sicker than ever, worse than when she'd left the hospital just two weeks before.

Watching as Lea took her in, Cleo's eyes hurried around the store, looking for the exit. The door was miles away from the green dresses. Cleo dropped the green purse with shaking hands, wrapping her hands tightly around the tomato plant frantically.

"It's okay," she whispers, her voice jumping up the octave, kissing the top of each leaf. "No one's hurting you. No one. You're safe right here with me."

"Mom, let's-"

Lea reached for Cleo, but Cleo pulled her arm away, bending down to pick up the purse from the floor and flinging it back over her shoulder. There was fear across Lea's face, all strength deteriorating as Cleo's emotions intensified.

"Do I need to call-?"

"I think we best be going," Cleo's voice constricted over her forced grin, teeth clenched.

"Thank you for your help."

Cleo stormed towards the exit, pushing back open the heavy door and running towards her bike. Lea raced behind her to the front door, lips poised open as if to shout before her mouth collapsed shut and let the door close between them.

There were tears in Cleo's eyes, but she didn't remember wanting to cry. She never cried, at least not without an occasion.

Cleo pushed the tomato plant down into the cupholder, confused about how it suddenly had become too big for the same container she had brought it in. She shoved it down into the cupholder harder, and more soil was lost to the sidewalk.

"It's just a green dress," Cleo murmured under her breath, ignoring the cautionary tale of the blinking red hand and racing across the intersection. "I've gotten myself into a tizzy over a *little green dress*."

Cleo took the path off the road the whole way this time, her hearing muffled, turning the entire world into a softened version of itself. Her vision remained blurry and inconsistent as she followed the cracks in the sidewalk back to her home.

The tightness in her chest made her forget the word she once used for this place, the place she'd run away from all those years ago. It was a cruel word; she'd said it when she threatened to never come back, but now, it escaped her completely.

She realized she'd left the front door open, the inside of the house uncomfortably humid. There wasn't any furniture in this room, only cardboard and scattered cushions with no structures to hold them.

Was this her place as it was? What about how she'd imagined it?

Looking up, Cleo realized the walls were sinking with the weight of the air, creating depressions against her shoulder as she slammed into the inside, attempting to push them up and out of her way. They were persistent. The room was too tight and would not move, and there was no way of reconstructing it.

This space no longer looked inviting but raggedy and outdated, with flies pooling across the walls and mismatched and broken wood across the floor.

Was this really where she lived?

Cleo crawled to her room, finding her clothes in their same disheveled state. At least this much was true. She threw the green purse down against the floor, scrambling her hands across each panel of fabric and holding them up to the skylight, none green or quite right.

"Do you think this matches?" Cleo asks the tomato plant, still clutched in her hand, waving frantically and uncoordinated. "What about this one?"

Falling to her knees, Cleo continued digging through the fabric, launching one thing after another into the air, revealing the lump of her family heirlooms concealed below her closet expedition; photos of her life in Bimini, Lea's second-grade class photo, and an expired rental ticket for diving gear. Cleo swept her hands through the floor's treasures, all her life's possessions of various shades and ages, turning up relics, but nothing green.

Cleo's phone rang, but she couldn't find it in the new mess she'd made. The vibration of the phone rattled underneath some impossible mass on the floor. Cleo reached around the canyons and buried her hands deep in the carpet, still coming up with everything besides what she was looking for. The room was too tight, constricting, and smaller and smaller until there was almost no space for Cleo or anything else.

The vibrating stopped.

Birds sang soft songs outside the window, almost like she was back in Bimini. Cleo hurried to the bathroom, hoping to catch a glimpse of them through her small window. She spied one in the tree just across from the way. It bounced along one of the branches, stopping only when it was perfectly eye-to-eye with her.

Its feathers were the perfect shade of green.

"Do you see that?" Cleo called, returning to the bedroom and picking up the tomato plant. There were indents on its small container where her hands had constricted around it, the plant crooked and uneasy, nearly falling out of the crushed pot.

"That bird is just the perfect thing, don't you think?" Cleo ran her fingers back over the leaves of the tomato plant, propping it back up in the bathroom window. The bird looked over, suddenly curious.

"Do you want to see it better?" Cleo asked the tomato plant. "Here, watch this," she lowered her voice, sharing yet another secret. "I know the best way to birdwatch."

She scurried back into her room and found the bag of birdseed at the bottom of her bookshelf, realizing its weight had knocked it over. Tearing into the bag, Cleo brought a fist full of seed with her back into the bathroom, sprinkling it all over the windowsill.

"Now you'll get to see it up nice and close."

Cleo pulled the window open, and after a moment of tender curiosity, the green feathered bird soared over, landing in the window and scavenging through the seed. Cleo squealed with delight. The bird hopped from seed to seed, quickly clearing the windowsill until it stood face-to-face with the tomato plant.

The bird cocked its head, eyes black, beady, and directionless, sprung its body forward, and pulled a tomato from the plant, leaving a slash across the stem.

"Hey!" Cleo shouted, eyes ripe with panic, trying to shoo the bird away. "Don't do that!"

The bird didn't answer but took another tomato.

"That's it," Cleo shouted, pulling the window down at full force, knocking the tomato plant out of the frame and towards the earth below. The bird stared at her blankly before diving down to the earth beneath, landing beside the plant. It looked back up at Cleo for a moment before continuing to eat.

"No!" Cleo's voice broke.

"Come back!"

The tomato plant didn't respond.

"Can't you hear me?" she shouted. "Get up! GET UP!"

Cleo turned around and brushed towards the bathroom door, stumbling back through her messy bedroom.

She'd get that bird. She'd *kill* that bird for what it had done.

Just as she reached for the door, in the corner of her eye, she spied it. A green dress was hidden beside a pair of cracked diving goggles and behind a binder stuffed with her discharge papers.

Grinning, she reached down, holding the garment up to the skylight. She couldn't believe she nearly missed it, almost having lost it in her frantic upheaval of the room.

It was perfect, exactly what she was looking for.

Cleo brushed her hands down the smooth fabric. It was so shiny she could see her reflection staring back at her. She looked beautiful against the green. It complemented her skin so well.

The dress was made for her. It had to have been.

Without a second thought, she held the dress tight to her body and stepped back into the bathroom to try it on.

ABOLITION

Curled under her green bed sheets with her phone in hand, Maya contemplated selling her virginity to a billionaire.

She'd read something about it being possible, maybe in a book or a TikTok comment, an article, a YouTube video, maybe?

She wasn't sure why the thought had reentered her mind, stumbling back into orbit among the sound of collisions of thunder and rain outside her window.

Maya couldn't remember the last time it had rained this hard and for this long, but perhaps the rattling of the thunder and lightning had made her think of the sound of rockets reentering the atmosphere, then space tourism, which led her brain back to the billionaires.

At seventeen, was it ethical for her to think about giving herself away to someone that made it big selling cheap plastic dog poop toys in China or child-slavery mineral mining?

It surely would have to be a weird experience. There was no way that people so open to the destruction of others were vanilla when it came to sex.

College is more expensive than ever, she thought, rolling over to her stomach. *Maybe it's not such a bad idea.*

Even still, Maya shuddered at the thought of having to piss on a bald billionaire, chalked the whole spiral up to an intrusive thought, and opened her phone. Some ideas were best not to follow.

Maya opened her phone to a video of a girl around her age getting asked to prom on the football field, blonde hair in a cascade of curls down her back, arms wrapping tightly around the neck of a football player, broad and smiling.

Hailey_2006xo was the username; a small circle profile picture hovering in the bottom corner detailed the pretty blonde girl being asked to prom in the video. She looked a bit familiar, but Maya couldn't place why.

Maya clicked on her profile. *Hailey Jacobs.*

"Cute," Maya let a puff of air float out of her nose. It was a bit funny. She'd seen promposal videos since middle school, and at this point, it felt like she had seen this very one before—several times. There were only so many ways to record yourself asking someone to prom, and Maya was convinced she'd seen all of them.

She left a like on the video, scratching the bridge of her nose while her unoccupied hand kept scrolling.

Beauty content, another stranger begging for money, a hot take nobody asked for, a surprise marriage proposal (fake), inflammatory news headline (surprisingly real), a video about a local lake running dry (unfortunately real), a recipe that turned flour into a chicken substitute (real?), a natural disaster in Cuba (real), a myth about an early human man breaking his femur and it healing being one of the defining signs of civilization and a desire to survive (real??), the rising unhoused population from out of control rent in the expanding city (very real), a woman pretending to be kidnapped and ending up in an underground box full of jelly beans (hopefully fake.)

After what felt like only a few moments, Maya's eyes darted away from the video to the clock in the upper right-hand corner of the screen. It was 3:45 am, and she'd need to be up for school in three hours.

Maya clicked her phone off and allowed the darkness to envelop the room. The rain had just begun to slow down, and the silence felt a bit foreign. Maya wasn't used to the quiet anymore; there had always been a way to make her experience a constant high of stimulation, which is what made falling asleep a challenge.

Instead, she tried to focus on the details still in her environment. The cicadas whirred in groups outside her window, each frequency passing as if part of an orchestra reading off sheet music. The moon was a hollowed-out crescent she could barely make out, as if someone had taken an ice cream scoop straight from the middle.

"Which billionaire do you think is into the most fucked up shit?"

Shaking her head, Maya's ears began to ring unpleasantly, so she focused on the five remaining glow-in-the-dark stars clinging for dear life on her ceiling, the last relics of childhood.

A corner peeled up on several sides of one, giving it less of the appearance of a star and more of a slightly illuminated gummy worm stuck to the ceiling.

She'd always liked having the stars there; they were easy to focus on when she couldn't sleep, often staring at them long enough to completely dissociate into slumber.

Maya had always found it more pleasant to be awake at night, with no interruptions and no interactions. She had free reign of the house as long as she was quiet enough to slip past her parent's bedroom door. She hadn't always liked being alone. It was just something that happened to Maya. Her friends moved away, her parents got stricter, and she grew older and more isolated.

She realized it might be better to be alone and find her interactions with the outside world in private spaces rather than public ones. You can't get embarrassed when you stare at people on the internet for too long, and you can't say the wrong thing when you have time to think of a cleverly worded comment.

Maya liked her bubble in that way, getting her school drama updates from classmates pouring their hearts out in a video recording, absorbing every word from the other side of a black screen, and watching tears come out of their eyes, smearing in their makeup. Sometimes, Maya would find herself crying with them.

Sleep eventually arrived after counting the folded corners of the star, eyes flickering between the collection of them on her ceiling.

The morning came the same way it always did, curtains pulled open by her mother, light stinging across her eyelids, clamoring for her phone on the nightstand or whenever she'd left it in bed. There's the small talk for breakfast, coffee in a thermos she'd made the night before, a curt goodbye to her parents, and a "good morning" to the bus driver.

Maya could chart the number of groundhog mornings she'd had, her mental checklist of scheduled interactions on pace for first period. Another day to get through before it was back to a nighttime of peace.

The day passed slowly, Maya stealing glimpses at her phone between classes in the hallway, eyes darting up only momentarily to avoid colliding with someone else doing the same thing. Her hands tingled and curled around her phone, the device warm in her hand like an extension of herself.

Another video appeared of two teenagers getting asked to prom (at the same time! *That was a new one*, she noted.), a therapist explaining the problem with trauma bonding, a baby tiger being reunited with its mother, another house flooding in Florida, twin sisters swap boyfriends, crop failure in the Midwest, an indie band begging for her to listen to their "song of the summer," a long lost pet returned to its original owner, a war crime committed in Russia, a baby saying its first words, more sanctions announced in Yemen after-

"Do you have a second to sign this petition about sending government support to Florida after the floods?"

Someone tapped her shoulder, and Maya's eyes darted up,

surprised by the sudden interaction. She blinked as her eyes adjusted from moving off the screen and realized it was the blonde girl from the video last night who got asked to prom. *Hailey_2006xo*, Maya almost replied but realized how insane that would be.

Hailey was just as beautiful in person as in the video; her hair in a curled ponytail down her back, blue fingernails on top of a clipboard stretched out to Maya. Hailey was smiling but serious, and Maya struggled to shove her phone into her jacket pocket.

Glancing down and back up, Maya was speechless but reached for the clipboard. Hailey gladly handed it over.

"Thanks for doing this." Hailey grinned. "We're trying to get all the attention on this we can."

Maya nods, swallowing the pit growing in her throat. Words were hard to find. She didn't have the space to think she was used to.

"I've seen all the videos," Maya nodded, her palm wet with sweat around the pen. "It looks awful."

"And that's just the stuff they're *showing* you," Hailey retorted, taking the clipboard and pen from Maya. "I have family there. You'll never believe how much of the coastline the ocean's destroyed. It's terrible we've let the climate get this out of control. Did you know oil companies could have done something about this as early as the eighties?"

Their fingers touched. Briefly.

Maya tried to memorize how smooth Hailey's skin felt.

When was the last time she'd made contact with anyone?

"No," Maya swallows, her throat heavy. "I-I didn't. That's terrible."

"Mhmm," Hailey nodded, reading back over the clipboard. "I don't think people are paying attention."

Remember to breathe. Remember to breathe, Maya reminded herself repeatedly, reciting the mantra and hoping it would calm her.

"Maya Malone," Hailey looked down, reading Maya's hurried handwriting off the clipboard. Hailey's teeth were pearly white, whiter than Maya imagined they'd be based on the video she'd seen. She couldn't take her eyes off them, hoping Hailey didn't close her mouth.

How do you even get your teeth to be *that white?* Maya wondered, running her tongue over her coffee-stained teeth, feeling suddenly insecure about her breakfast for the last three years. She'd have to see if Hailey had a teeth care video on her page.

"I don't think I've seen you around her before." Hailey narrowed her eyebrows, frowning. Her glowing teeth disappeared behind pursed full lips.

"Oh, I, I've been here," Maya answered. "I'm just doing my own thing, I guess. You know? It do be like that." The internet-eese slips out of her mouth before she realized and she wished she could swallow all the word vomit back down her throat, along with her whole existence. She was sure this couldn't be how interactions were supposed to work.

To her surprise, Hailey laughed. "You're right. It *do* be like that."

It was as if all the background noise had disappeared from the hallway, Hailey's laugh the only thing that reverberated between Maya's ears. It was clear and bright, as glowing as her blonde hair underneath the cool fluorescent lights of the school. Maya wished she could bottle it, store it somewhere she could hear it all the time, over and over.

"Do you have TikTok or Insta?" Hailey asks. "It's always cool to talk to people who seem to care about what's happening."

The scene had turned distinctly dreamlike, Hailey's outline hazy and almost indiscriminate, as if still appearing in front of Maya on screen. Maya managed to nod, giving her username to Hailey, who looked her up immediately.

"Oh, cool, you're already following me." Hailey peered down at her phone, and Maya braced for the sudden questions about why, but none of them came.

"We have some mutuals. I swear everyone we go to school with comes up on my For You Page, which is only slightly embarrassing. A bit like being in the school hallway all the time, don't you think?"

"For sure," replied Maya, feigning confidence under the wave of excitement in her belly as she felt her phone vibrating in her hand.

"Anyway, thanks for signing the petition. I'll see you around!" said Hailey, walking towards the next wave of students behind Maya. "Bye, Maya!"

Already looking down at her phone, Maya grinned.

Hailey_2006xox is now following you.

Before she knew it, it was 3:45 am, and Maya was still scrolling through Hailey's page.

Maya had learned so much about her. She was in the debate club and Model United Nations. It seemed like Hailey had gone to East Lake High School as long as Maya had. She did have a teeth care routine video, lots of whitening strips, and, as Maya guessed, no coffee.

Maya mapped her family tree in shared last names in her "Following" tab and found out her mother was a philanthropist and her father a pastor. Her brother attended Cornell, and her baby sister was starting Kindergarten next year (an oops baby, Maya assumed), giggling as if involved in the inner circle of family gossip.

Hailey was passionate about climate change, often reposting and making detailed videos about the heightened danger they were all in if they didn't get their act together. Maya felt emboldened by Hailey's confidence and intellect, quickly following several organizations Hailey cited as having made a difference. She'd like to be able to talk to Hailey again, this time more prepared. Maya took mental notes over each video, filing the information in a growing note on her phone.

Maya had to stop herself from saving every video she could find of Hailey laughing, her full smile and ringing laugh fixed in her brain and giving her a rush of dopamine every time she heard it. She played the prom video again, watching the boy, *08sherms36*, asking Hailey to prom and her saying yes, over and over and over.

Maya imagined the experience through Hailey's eyes, looking up at someone who wanted to take her to the dance and around at a crowd cheering for them. Before she realized it, she saw the experience inversely, being the one Hailey was smiling back at. Heat rose in Maya's face and chest until something small landed on her face.

A single ceiling star.

Morning arrived on schedule, with open curtains, curt parent conversations, another bus ride, but this time, a green juice for breakfast and one of her mom's protein bars. No coffee.

Based on Hailey's recent posts, Maya knew she could catch her once she arrived at the school bus loop. Hailey had posted several videos the last few days, standing outside the school during the morning arrival, asking people for signatures on her Florida petition. If Maya had learned anything – and she had learned quite a lot about Hailey – she was incredibly consistent.

Maya spotted her from the bus window, golden waves down her back just a few feet before her. Courage bolstered her body.

She knew everything she needed to know about Hailey now–her favorite coffee shop, where she liked to hang out with her friends, all her favorite songs from the radio, and her sense of humor.

Maya cataloged through the mental insights she'd spent the last twelve hours collecting, Hailey's personality coming together in gray text blurbs and between disaster scenes from across the world that she'd reshared. Hailey was compassionate like that and was well-connected. Hailey was impressed by Maya yesterday, and today she'd be impressed by her too.

There was no way that she wouldn't be prepared now.

"Hailey!" Maya called, waving her hand in the air, throwing her words into the whirring of teenagers pushing their way towards the front gate. Hailey turned around; eyebrows furrowed before she spied Maya in the distance. She couldn't recall the last time she'd yelled that loud.

"Oh, hey, May!"

Maya swallowed.

"Maya," her voice felt hollow.

Hailey shook her head, "Right, I'm so sorry! How are you?"

"I'm well," Maya recharged her energy, focusing on the end goal, connecting with Hailey. She struggled to catch her breath, stopping herself from racing through all the words she'd had lined up in her head since the early morning hours. Like a stage play, the curtain was rising, and this was a performance, a delicate one. She had to be graceful.

"I saw the video you posted about Florida yesterday. It looks awful out there."

Solid opening line.

Hailey took a heavy breath, "Absolutely devastating. I've been trying to get as many people to see what's happening. I think so many people our age get-"

"Caught up in their own worlds," Maya sighed, studying Hailey's face for an agreeable response. She provided one, a half smile, soft eyes, and a nod.

"I couldn't have said it better myself."

Maya's heart nearly exploded out of her chest, the ringing racing to her ears.

"I think it's cool how you're doing Model UN. I think I'd like to work in government someday too," said Maya.

A bold-faced lie, but Maya was high off the attention.

Maya had no idea what she wanted to do. Maya knew nothing about herself right now, only that this was the best she'd felt in years. The most *real* she'd felt in years, her hands reattached to her body, her mind sensing what the present was, not what was presented to her behind a glass panel.

"Really?" Hailey smiled, pearly white. "That's amazing. You should join us sometime."

"Yeah?" Maya's heart reentered the atmosphere, another sonic boom.

Is this what it felt like to go to space?

"Definitely. We meet on Thursdays after school in the

social sciences building."

"Cool, I'll-I'll be there!" said Maya, grinning.

Maybe this is why billionaires do it.

"Amazing," Hailey pulled her phone out of her pocket, checking the time.

"We should get to first period. Maybe I'll catch you later?"

"Sure," Maya grinned.

Hailey waved goodbye and left in the opposite direction. Maya was planted still on the grass of the bus loop, the sea of fellow high schoolers parting and flowing into the building without her. She found herself wishing she'd recorded the interaction, wanting to look back and see the enthusiasm and shine across Hailey's face over and over again.

The bell rang, and Maya submerged herself in the crowd of students rushing into the hallway.

This had to be what it felt like to get high. Maya needed another hit, another positive interaction with Hailey, another like. She pulled her phone from her pocket, researching as much as she could find about what was happening in Florida, studying every opinion, every action plan. She'd be prepared to talk to Hailey about any of it. Maybe she'd even get to tell Hailey something she didn't already know.

Maya overflowed at the thought, fingers dancing across the keyboard as she frantically took more notes on the situation, how many people had died, how many homes had been affected, the inadequacy of the government, and the map of the buildings doomed to take on water next.

It was horrifying to look at, Maya realized as she tapped through each video. There had been so many warnings about building close to the ocean, many people had begged the city for better infrastructure, and so many scientists had called for radical change before it was too late, but now, it was.

"People are just…caught up in their own shit," a crying woman sobbed on Maya's screen. "This is *real*. This is happening *now*. And you may not be living in it yet, but you will be."

Biting down on her lip, Maya stared at the woman on

screen, tanned dark from the South Florida sun, a small boy balanced on the top of her hip. Her teeth were not pearly white, and she didn't smile. Maya couldn't get herself to like the video, the woman's words echoing between her ears as she scrolled past it.

During first period, Maya balanced her phone on top of her leg, just out of her teacher's eye line, going back to scrolling through Hailey's comment section, looking for any semblance of how she might respond to any of the talking points Maya had in mind. She read them softly to herself, mouthing the words while imagining what it might be like to someday appear in the photos and videos alongside Hailey.

Chewing her bottom lip, she memorized the accounts Hailey was following, tapping her hand anxiously on the top of her desk. She was nearly jumping out of her skin, transfixed on every word, studying the cadence in which Hailey typed. Her heart fluttered as she came across new clues and new interactions, her head buzzing with the novel information.

"Maya," her teacher called upfront. "Can you bring your phone up here, please? You need to be working."

Maya's heart dropped, her teeth pressing so hard into her top lip that the taste of blood nearly overpowered the anxiety settling in her stomach as she stood up and shyly set her phone down on the teacher's desk.

"Thank you," she replied. "Focus on your work. You can pick this up from me at the end of the day."

Suddenly feeling completely naked and exposed, Maya was left with her thoughts for the first time since imagining selling her virginity to a billionaire two nights ago.

And you may not be living in it yet, but you will be. The desperate woman's voice rattled around Maya's head, eyes wide, hair in knots from the constant wind and rain. The desperation tightened Maya's throat.

"Think about the assignment," Maya insisted, looking down at the numbers on her math test but seeing through them to some impossible screen. She imagined herself in Hailey's pictures, or maybe, being the one recording the scene of her

and the boy asking her to prom, or maybe, Maya was asking her to prom instead. But they were in Florida this time, and it was not Hailey she was with, but the woman from the video, desperate and shaking Maya by the shoulders.

"This is happening now," the woman repeated over and over again until it became a drone barely audible above the crashing sound of the ocean.

More rain was coming, but the rest of the United States *wasn't* coming. This is going to be it, the end.

Maya winced, and suddenly she was in her childhood bedroom, Hailey's hand running down the outside of her leg, hundreds of ceiling stars enveloping them in a dichotomous, glowing darkness. There's a billionaire in the corner, watching, waiting, phone in hand to film.

Her parents opened the curtains, but the night was still black outside, and the scene distorted back into the classroom.

Maya knew how to turn flour into a chicken alternative but couldn't imagine speaking to anyone in this room. How would she even know what to say? There was no script, no guidelines, and no predictable outcomes. More impossible images blur together, her mind a kaleidoscope of natural disasters, DIY projects, and screaming politicians, but they all had Hailey's laugh, *every single one.*

"Stop!" Maya shouted at the loudest volume she could remember in recent daylight.

"Maya," her teacher's voice was firm. "You're being incredibly disruptive. Do you need to see a guidance counselor?"

"I-" Maya swallowed. "No, I'm fine. Sorry."

The math problems blurred together, so Maya scribbled *IDK* at the top of her paper and waited for the bell to ring. Like every morning, it arrived on schedule, and she hurried out of the classroom and into the flooded hallway.

There would be no escape to a screen today, only the pimple-y, sweating, curious-eyed gazes of her classmates and returning to her own consciousness.

Maya scanned the hallway for Hailey, a familiar face in a

sea of people she's only seen on screens. She spied people she knew had broken up with their partners recently, two friends giggling at their locker she knew were talking shit on their spam accounts about each other yesterday, two boys facing opposite directions trying to conceal their blushed grins in the other's presence. For as little time as Maya looked at these people, she felt as if she knew all of them so intimately here, seeing their parted lips and heavy eyes, all the same as they were on screen.

"You're Maya, right?"

There was a tap on her shoulder. A short girl with wire-framed glasses and acne, pale with apprehension, looked up at her.

Scanning the entirety of her brain for recognition, Maya came up with nothing. She'd never seen this girl before, not once, not anywhere.

"Yeah," Maya answered. She became overwhelmed by the busyness of the hallway, and habitually, she reached for her phone, temporarily forgetting its absence, which sent her heart rate skyrocketing.

"I just wanted to see if you were alright. I'm in your first-period math class, and you seemed kind of... off."

Maya didn't answer right away, looking around the hallway for Hailey, but there was still no sight of her. Hours must have passed in the time she'd been standing out here. If only she just had her phone, then she could check, see what Hailey was looking at, where she'd been last, if she'd gone somewhere else, if she'd forgotten entirely about Maya.

"I'm fine," Maya answered curtly, trying not to look the girl in the eyes.

"You know," the girl continued, barely audible over the bustling noise. "I really can't stand all the people in here, and it's so busy I- I feel like I can't have an original thought."

For the first time in years, Maya's brain took pause.

There was understanding, and at least for a moment, the images of implanted memories from other people's experiences and third-person perspectives of the end of the world didn't overwhelm her consciousness. Maya felt unbound to silence, to a chronic study of life rather than the experience of it.

At this moment, the need to soak in reality through another channel stopped.

"Really?" Maya asked.

"Really. I don't think people realize-"

"-how isolating the noise is," Maya finished the girl's sentence but realized that it was her own thought she'd completed, not a prompt.

The girl laughed differently than Hailey, more nasally, with more of her gums showing from underneath her thin lips. Her teeth were stained yellow. "Jinx," the girl grinned.

"I'm Cassandra."

"Maya."

"I know."

ORDER

The kid was in the shower for over an hour.

Nathan had tried to be personable by offering him the bathroom first, eyeing the sweat pooling on the bridge of the boy's brow, complexion red with embarrassment.

Though the boy easily towered over him, his face was still flush with a youth Nathan hadn't seen in his reflection for years.

"Go ahead," Nathan gestured towards the open bathroom door. "I'll watch TV or something."

"Thanks," the boy remarked, breathlessly stepping inside and locking the door behind him.

Nathan picked a bed on the right near the window, and plopped down to flick through the hotel channels mindlessly. Nothing was on anymore, and Nathan couldn't think of the last time he'd watched TV and found something he was interested in. Hotel channels were especially sterile, mostly infomercials and repeats of movies from decades ago. God forbid a kid wake up in the middle of the night and turn on the TV to something realistic.

The day had been long, tedious, and uncomfortable. As much as Nathan had been told about how MEPS worked for military recruitment, nothing had prepared him for the lines of people, countless tests, and excessive questions he'd been asked throughout the day.

Have you ever been married? No.

Any problems with drug or alcohol abuse? No.

How tall are you? Five six.

Are there any underlying medical conditions? No.

How old are you? Twenty-four.

Why are you enlisting?

Nathan hadn't been sure about the last one, studying how his shoe fit in the square tile on the floor as the woman with a tight hair bun tapped her fingers quietly on her clipboard. She was eyeing him, and he could feel it, but he couldn't look up at her. He'd never been keen on looking people in the eyes.

Shifting his foot just to the left, the front of his toes buckled outside the lines of the tile square, barely too big.

"I'd like to serve my country," Nathan finally replied, settling on the most appropriate answer. He twisted his shoe back in the square, this time at a slight angle, the border of the tile now clear on all sides.

Nathan heard the shower running through the hotel room wall, barely audible over the evening news he'd let buzz on the TV.

War was bubbling up throughout Eastern Europe, record heat waves scorching most of the African continent. Another famous man in Hollywood had cheated on his wife, trading their shared skyscraper for solo adventures to some dive jazz bar downtown.

The newscasters stared blankly into the camera, reading off the teleprompter and swiftly moving from story to story as if none of them warranted an additional thought. The way they flipped between events was disorienting enough to make you forget about the last as if none of them mattered.

Still, Nathan didn't mind the TV so long as he treated

it like background noise, as he turned his attention out the window towards the flurry of people coming in and out of the hotel lobby: couples with children, a woman and her small dog, and a man holding a folded open book; the painting and its cast of characters unfurled itself against the urban backdrop, each character taking their respective places in the frame. There was something relaxing about watching people conduct themselves in their activities, even when Nathan would much rather stay sprawled out in the hotel bed than go anywhere else.

Watching from this distance gave him a separation from the different lives outside, but enough of a glimpse into it to make him feel like he was still somehow part of it. He wondered about what these people's lives might look like, the jobs they commuted to on the weekdays, what they liked to do in their free time, if they had any fears, if they had something they'd die for.

Nathan wondered how often people thought about things in the way that he did, as an ongoing stream of different prompts with brief and prepared answers, without space for the unplanned, without wavering from old decisions. It wasn't something he often talked about with other people, if at all, how there was no going back the other way when he'd cornered his mind.

The shower stopped, sputtering out its last stream of water, and went silent. There was the sound of footsteps and swinging legs up and over the side of the tub. The sink turned on, then off again.

Nathan kicked off his shoes he hadn't realized he was still wearing and let them fall off at the bottom of the bed. He was exhausted, though he felt like he hadn't done much of anything today.

Maybe standing in lines, having conversations about himself with strangers, and demonstrating his character, felt more strenuous to him than it would for other people. Perhaps this was another thought about himself he wasn't sure if other people had, that discussions with other people were often overly tiring and not worth the extra energy it took for him to have them. He'd found over time, the best versions of himself came out of plenty of quiet and space, where his thoughts could meander with just his own, without interruption.

Besides, he'd certainly not talked to as many people as he had today in a while, even while working at the Home Depot down the road from his parent's house. It wasn't like his conversations at Home Depot were about him. Strangers would approach him and ask questions, but most didn't require well-thought-out answers, only aisle numbers, price references, and promising to "check the back."

Nathan liked his Home Depot job, but not enough to stay. It had been a compromise posed to his parents after getting his GED following dropping out of high school, a compromise for putting them through the embarrassment of having a son that hadn't done things the right way.

School had never come easy to Nathan. He'd struggled through math and science, the formulas blended together into some kind of number soup on his paper, quickly pushed from his brain before he reached the question at the bottom of the page.

He hadn't liked the social element of school much either, being asked to participate in group projects or attending school-sponsored events. Nathan didn't like the whispering in the crowded hallways or the perceptions he knew his classmates had of him, the quiet kid. Even if they didn't say anything to him, he swore he could feel their eyes peering into the back of his head as he sat down each day to eat lunch or when he pulled books from his locker.

They were always watching, making checklists, and tallying up all the ways he'd never blend in with the rest of them. He was The Outsider. The Stranger. The Unlike.

Nathan didn't like any of it – the people, the pressure, the constant rushing from place to place. It was more than school, he now realized. The world also moved in bustling hallways, only more crowded and with more sets of eyes waiting, watching for something new and foreign to observe, hungry to cast him further as The Other.

Now that he thought of it, Nathan didn't know what he liked. He'd always felt like nothing satisfied him and brought him overt joy. There was always something wrong, and he knew it; even when he'd rev himself up with anticipation or let himself get genuinely excited, every moment Nathan felt he should be happy in fell utterly flat. He was never an active participant in his own joy, only showing up as a critic to take it away from even himself.

Nathan realized that there was only one honest answer to the question he'd been asked earlier:

Why are you enlisting? It was the only thing left to do.

The bathroom door swung open, and the boy walked out into the hotel room wearing his pajamas, clutching a book and got into the bed opposite Nathan's. His shoulders were hunched over as if protecting himself in some kind of shell; his thin back rounded over the book clasped against his narrow chest.

"Sorry that took so long," the boy murmured, pulling back the bed's comforter and lying down. "I didn't realize how sweaty I was."

"Don't worry about it," Nathan replied, peeling off his socks and shoving them into his shoes. "I was just enjoying the nightly news."

The boy laughed, though Nathan didn't think he'd said anything funny.

"A whole lot of nothing on again," the boy remarked. "More corporate-sponsored nonsense."

The TV flashed an ad for women's multivitamins and another for investing in collectible gold coins before returning to coverage of the war in Eastern Europe.

"We come to you tonight just south of the frontlines with reporter David Jesup. David, can you hear us, okay?"

"Thanks, Anna, yes I can. It's another tense day of fighting and negotiations here-"

"You think we're gonna get involved in that?" the boy asked Nathan, his eyes flickering between the Eastern

European countryside flashing across the tv screen and the freckled green carpet of the hotel. Both landscapes were similar shades of green. The boy twisted his foot into the carpet.

Nathan shrugged.

The boy studied the indents his foot made on the floor, ruffling up the edges of the carpet and smoothing it back into place over and over again.

"It would suck to be sent over there."

"I can think of a few places that would probably be worse."

"Like where?" The boy sat up, intrigued. The TV returned to a commercial for men's erectile dysfunction medication, followed by a reminder for next week's Sunday Night Football game.

Nathan frowned, racking his mind for what he knew about current global conflicts or places that would be uncomfortable to live in. He'd watched videos about a surprising amount of them, tattered villages with unwalled buildings, deserts with unbelievable amounts of heat, cities without water infrastructure, island nations with disappearing coastlines and no natural resources.

There were many places to be where war wasn't the worst part of them.

It was being human.

"Probably the Middle East. Shallow islands in the Pacific. Parts of Africa. A bunch of places they don't want outsiders involved."

"It looks like they don't want us there either," the boy frowned, watching the newscaster duck his head down behind a broken building wall, lowering his head at the sound of gunshots, eyes staring directly into the camera.

Nathan shrugged.

The boy shuffled underneath the peach-colored comforter. His collarbones were visible near the top of his navy-colored shirt, his face still broad with baby fat. Concealed by the covers, he looked no older than thirteen.

"I'm hoping if I get through Basic early enough, I'll get stationed somewhere else before things kick off over there," the boy rambled, hands knotted together above the covers, his voice and hands betraying the confidence in his words.

Nathan nodded, picked up his shoes, and moved them to a neat position by the front door. He'd always kept his shoes away from the bed—too many germs.

"What about you?"

Nathan came out from around the corner, folding his arms flat across his chest. "What about me?"

"What are you trying to do? Where do you want to get stationed?"

Nathan frowned. He'd never considered where he might like to be stationed or what he'd like to do as a job once he enlisted. During the meetings with recruiters, they'd told him he'd done surprisingly well enough on his ASVAB to have his pick of the available contracts. He'd settled on infantry without giving the others a second look. It had been easy, he hadn't had to think about it, and no one had pushed him to reconsider. No one had to.

"*Tenophine may be able to help treat your mild to moderate depression symptoms. Ask your doctor about it today!*" The TV whispered.

"Maybe out west somewhere," replied Nathan. "I'd like to see Washington."

"I love Washington!" the boy replied. "My parents and I took a trip this last summer for my graduation. I'm hoping to go out that way too, and then once my contract is finished, start school out there or something."

The boy looked immediately less tense, looking out across the hotel room as if he were somewhere else entirely. Nathan watched as the boy relaxed back into the bed.

"How old are you?"

"Eighteen," the boy responded a bit sheepishly. "As of last Thursday."

Nathan looked him over, the coyness in his expression, the fixed part of his gaze. He couldn't believe how young he looked. He could barely remember being that old, sinking through the high school hallways, celebrating his eighteenth in his mother's car on the way home from his GED test. The world had still felt so broad at eighteen, ripe with possibility, even if Nathan hadn't been entirely sure what that possibility was. Now, too much time had passed to feel that way, the world narrowing with every birthday, every hour he'd spent wandering, floating aimlessly between days.

Eighteen was still young enough to pick what tethered you down.

"A fatal car accident has killed recent college graduate Elliot Wilde. Wilde flipped his truck after running a yellow light-"

"Why not start school now?" Nathan asked the boy, sitting on the corner of the bed and turning down the TV.

The boy furrowed his eyebrows. "What do you mean?"

"Why enlist and wait to go to school in Washington if it's what you want to be doing?"

The boy frowned.

"I don't know, the loans? The distance? At least enlisting, I know I'll have food and somewhere to sleep."

Nathan nodded in understanding. "Sure, but how much will you get to decide for yourself?"

"A local lake is running dry, Gary Martinez investigates the reports that it was once a prehistoric watering hole—"

The boy flipped the pages of the book clutched in his hands, fidgeting. "Do you care about that? Deciding for yourself what you do? Where you go?"

"Not particularly," Nathan replied. "But I'm not eighteen."

The boy closed the book and laid it on the nightstand. *The Castle* by Frank Kafka. The blue cover stood out in contrast with the plain dark wood dresser. He didn't say anything and turned his eyes toward the TV screen.

"There's a new way to fight off aging; with Klem Age Rewind, turn back the clock on wrinkles and get your best years out of the rearview mirror."

"These ads get more and more absurd," Nathan frowned. "I think I know more about women's skincare than the war."

The boy looked down at the peach comforter.

"Me too."

Before returning to the news anchor, the TV buzzed through several commercials, pet food, cloud-powered storage, home security cameras, a pro-cop crime show, and the latest diet medication.

"For our final story tonight, we're Remembering the Fallen. A tribute to American Hero Franklin Hernandez. A Desert Storm leader died today after a four-year battle with brain cancer. Hernandez dedicated his life to American work in the Middle East, helping countless soldiers navigate the world of living a world away from the comforts of home while promoting a diplomatic relationship with those abroad. He was forty-one."

A photo of Franklin came on screen, an American flag overlaid on his army uniform. His eyes were concealed behind dark black sunglasses against the background of the desert. Nathan always found it strange to show pictures of the dead while they were alive as if that same body wasn't now lying still and unmoving. It was too much like watching a ghost.

"Thanks for joining us tonight. We'll be back tomorrow."

There was a moment of darkness on screen. Nathan and the boy spied themselves on the unlit black background of the TV. Both looked into the warped screen; even sitting in bed, the boy still towered over Nathan. A pair of shadowed dark eyes met an unframed pair of blue ones on the TV; Nathan and the boy made eye contact for the first time.

Suddenly, the screen flooded with a vibrant yellow background, and a puppet introduced the audience to a high blood pressure medication.

"I don't think I can do this." The boy said softly. He'd wrapped his hands back up underneath the blanket.

"Then don't," Nathan replied, facing the boy.

"If you want to be somewhere else, don't go."

The boy's face was full of fear but also a decisiveness Nathan had never seen, even on himself.

"Can I really just…leave?"

Nathan nodded. "You can."

The boy paused, looking around at the small hotel room before pulling the comforter off and standing up. His bare feet sunk into the grass green carpet.

"I'm gonna text my mom," said the boy, reaching down and grabbing the book off the nightstand. He looked back at Nathan.

"Are you gonna stay?"

Nathan's eyes shifted between the boy and the vibrant hues of the TV.

He thought about his father, the neighborhood he grew up in, and the smell of the Home Depot. He thought about high school, linoleum tiles and the smell of floor cleaner, floating in a crowded sea of people, his bedroom with a closed door, dark curtains, the wrinkles around his mother's eyes, a failed test, birthday candles, going on a jog, sunrise.

"I am," Nathan replied.

"Okay."

The boy nodded and returned to the bathroom with his small duffel bag. A bottle of toothpaste and a toothbrush get dropped inside. The sink turned on and off again, though, faster this time.

When the boy returned from the bathroom, his cheeks had more color. The boy slung the bag over his right shoulder and held Kafka in his left hand. He had kept his pajamas on.

The boy took a deep breath.

"Thank you," the boy said, slipping on his sneakers.

"I'm not sure I did much of anything," Nathan shrugged.

"Just let you think out loud, I guess."

"Just, thank you."

The boy put his other shoe on and scanned the room for anything he might have left behind before reaching for the door handle.

"I'm Joseph," the boy said.

"Nathan."

"Thank you, Nathan." Joseph pulled open the door to the hotel room, letting in a stream of cold air from the hallway.

"Maybe I'll run into you in Washington."

Nathan managed a smile. "Maybe you will."

Joseph returned the grin, stepped out into the hallway, and let the door fall closed behind him. The TV continued to hum in disorganized soundbites before Nathan finally turned it off.

The room was silent beyond the shuffling of several feet in the room above him. Nathan stood up from the bed, walking back over to the window just in time to catch Joseph walking out of the lobby doors and into the parking lot towards an idling car. His mother climbed out of the front seat, grabbed him, and pulled him in close to her. She might have been crying, or laughing. Nathan was too far away to tell, but seeing it was still nice.

Nathan closed the curtains and walked to the bathroom, glad to finally have a shower.

CHANGE

The cooling soup on the table, a beacon of simplicity, disappointed Diane more than usual that night.

The soup was surrounded by warm bread she'd purchased from the market earlier that day. It had curls of rosemary leaves strung across the top in a beautiful fixed pattern. Still, without the bustling of busy hands racing to eat, the soup looked overcrowded by the bread. Perhaps she'd just put too much on the plate.

Diane heard the TV in a low hum, a talk show of bickering men behind closed doors. Her husband Emmett usually ate in his room, not without first coming out and supplying her with a firm yet compassionate kiss on the forehead before retreating to his cave.

Lately, however, Emmett had been less concerned with emerging from the depths of his room, the rowdy words of angry men on talk shows warded off only by a closed door.

Diane tried not to mind. After preparing dinner and setting the table, she'd wait forty-five minutes to see if Emmett would emerge from his quarters before packing him a plate, covering it with a thin piece of tin foil, and placing it on the top shelf of the fridge.

Her fingers, thin and made unidentifiable from cleaning products that had erased any semblance of a fingerprint, pushed the tin foil down under the bottom of the plate and signed the top with a sharpie and a small heart. The following day, she'd usually find the dirty dish in the sink and any leftovers half-thrown in the trash can.

Still, she didn't think she *really* minded. It was good that Emmett was eating. He worked long hours and spent much of his time wrangling unruly students as a high school dean.

Diane knew that sometimes moments of peace just couldn't be shared.

Still, Diane couldn't help but feel particularly disappointed about the abandoned soup on the table tonight. The bread, made by a local store in the quaint downtown, was buttered and salted, and though her hands ached, she'd cut it into triangle-sized bites that were perfect for dipping.

Now, after a few hours of sitting out, the bread had begun to look less and less spectacular than it had when she'd first picked it up, blending in as if it was part of the room, not something special.

Diane had been so excited to go to the shop that afternoon and pick up the bread. She'd requested it that day so she could pick it up fresh, calling first thing in the morning to make sure they got her order in for the day.

Feeling incredibly nervous, she'd driven slowly down the central road downtown, handicap tag swinging in the mirror as she bounced down the brick road. It had been a long time since she'd come down this far into the city, but she was excited to do it. Driving had become increasingly difficult the last few years, but she would not let it deter her today. Today was special. She had the energy to do something above and beyond the normal, hoping Emmett's peace could be shared with her while breaking bread.

Finding a spot just across the road from the bakery, Diane locked the car, raising her head as she walked towards the shop. She took a deep breath to steady herself, searching for confidence with every footstep.

She was surprised by the disarray she'd found the once-bustling downtown strip. The grocery store that once neighbored the bakery now boasted boarded-up windows, and the clothing store lights flickered. The street had only a few cars shuffled indiscriminately between each of the businesses. It looked as if the whole downtown was in hibernation, waiting for something to happen.

Though it was November, it was unseasonably warm. Diane discarded her pale gray scarf in the bottom of her deep handbag. She'd always worn that scarf when she went downtown; it was one of the nicest things she owned. But now, the way it trapped the afternoon heat against her skin was nearly insufferable.

The bell on the door rang upon Diane's arrival, shouting with pings that echoed throughout the store. Though she looked around for the shopkeeper, the room was otherwise vacant.

A small TV buzzed on the top of the counter, recounting the record-breaking heat wave across the city. Diane felt increasingly foolish in her winter attire, resisting the urge to remove her coat. This was another record-breaking warm day, for, as Diane now learned for the first time, the eighth year in a row.

She also learned though it was growing warmer here, it was nothing compared to many other parts of the world. Diane watched as the TV cycled through multiple images of battered children and families migrating from their home countries, arms full of a lifetime's worth of possessions in search of more seasonable weather. It had grown so hot that many had died in the streets as the riverbeds ran completely dry, including one of the city's most important lakes. She watched as the news quickly recounted the number of deaths before switching to a program about a record-breaking tour for one of the world's biggest pop artists who had just put a payment down for her tenth home.

This news didn't at all sound like the disgruntled men arguing on Emmett's TV, those who dug their heels in the sand for the civil liberties she'd grown up with, the old ways, at least, that's what she made out from the other side of the door. They bickered through their cycle of conversational topics, warned to be wary of the media as if they weren't also part of it. Diane would sit quietly on the other side of the door before giving up and returning to her book. She didn't want any part in these conversations, but as she finally took her coat off and draped it over her arm, it seemed there was no longer an escape.

Diane noticed a bag on a shelf at the side of the store with her name on the tag that said: "For Pickup." She placed her hands around the bottom of the bag and found it was still warm. It must have just come out of the oven. She waited a bit longer, hoping to run into the baker and thank him for taking her last-minute order, but no one emerged.

She left fifteen dollars on the counter and walked back to her car.

Maybe this was the reason for her disappointment tonight, she wondered, swirling her spoon around in the tomato soup. This was the first time in a long time she had interacted with the world and returned with something worth sharing.

Worth sharing with Emmett.

The bread looked so beautiful on the plate, so intricate. Diane wished there had been someone in the shop that she could talk to, learn what kind of flour they used, how they carved such an intricate design in the top of the loaf, and teach her about something new. Instead, she felt full of more questions than answers, beyond the bread, beyond the uncrowded downtown, beyond the heat.

Had the world changed that much since she'd last stepped into it?

Maybe she had seen things changing but chose not to *really* take notice of them. Her garden needed more water than ever, the heavy blanket of summer becoming harder to pull off each year, weighing down all the flowers in the yard.

Her neighbor's trees had hardly any yellow or red leaves, the traditional waving flag for the changing seasons. These silent reflections were always kept to herself, filed away under other misattributions she'd not vocalized.

Everything was simply the way it was. It had to be.

Or did it?

Diane wondered, looking down at the table towards the soup.

Hurrying to the kitchen, Diane approached one of the taller cabinets and pulled down a small white bowl and matching plate. She carried them back to the table, losing her balance and bumping her head on the wall.

Disregarding the dizziness and tiny black dots pooling in her vision, she felt her way back toward the table as her vision began to clear. She'd done this same trek before; this house had the same hallways since she and Emmett had married so many decades ago. Diane curled her fingers around the head of the wooden chair, steadying herself with one hand and raising a ladle to the bowl in the other.

She filled the bowl with soup, gently placing four neat slices of bread around it. She laid a metal spoon in the bowl, took a deep breath, and walked towards Emmett's office.

It had been a while since she'd returned here, and that became clearer as she approached the door looming in the distance. The hallway had grown tight with Emmett's books, mismatched and discarded clothing, and empty boxes and bags containing products from Amazon. It was almost as if his cave had grown beyond the office, now encroaching into the hallway, something else, Diane realized, she hadn't noticed.

Diane curled her feet together to squeeze through the tight space, the bickering noise from Emmett's videos growing louder the closer she got to the front door. The soup bowl was so hot that her fingers burned from the underside of the plate, wobbling as she navigated the foreign passage. She felt a familiar tinge of nervousness in her stomach as she took a deep breath like she was back downtown with a scarf that had grown too hot.

Finally, the door loomed directly in front of her as she wrapped both hands tightly around the small white plate. Looking down at the bowl and bread, she noticed more of the intricacies in the rosemary leaves strewn out across the slices. She'd tried to preserve the bread's design the best she could as she was slicing it into pieces, hoping that, just maybe, Emmett would appreciate it as much as she had.

Maybe she'd ask him what he thought of the bread. Or perhaps, about the downtown.

Had he heard how much it had changed recently? How many businesses had folded?

Or maybe she'd ask him about the state of the world. Ask him about the people escaping the heat she'd seen on the news. Ask if he'd noticed how often she'd had to water the garden the last few years. Ask him if he'd noticed the changes the way she had. Ask if he'd noticed her.

"Perhaps that is the greatest question," Diane heard the booming voice of a loud young man through the door. "What do we do about climate migrants, and how do we keep them where *they* belong, in their own homes, not ours. The elitist hoax being sold to everyday citizens is about *your* civil liberties and the right to live a life of your own. Do you *really* want that kind of change?"

Diane frowned.

What she'd seen on the TV in the bakery today had looked real enough to her, real enough to warrant some kind of change. There were children in those photos, cheeks hollow and skin burnt dark. Children that, in another timeline, could have very well been her own.

After another moment of indiscriminate commentary and laughter, Diane heard the video pause and a creak from Emmett's chair. Only a moment later, he swung open the door, looking down at her.

His broad face has worn with age; dark bags hung around both his eyes, neck wide, and skin translucent. It had been a long time since Diane had truly tried to take in her husband, and at this moment, she realized just how different he looked too. Almost hollow.

"What is it?" Emmett asked, looking between her and the bowl of soup.

"I-" Diane stumbled over her words, the questions she'd prepared, the script she'd settled on, all running absent from her head. All she could think about was how much the bowl burned in her hands.

"I made dinner."

Emmett smirked. "Finally, I'm starving."

He lifted the plate and bowl from Diane's hands, and she breathed in a sigh of relief just as Emmett closed the door.

THIGHS

Where there had once been only three houses peering over the lake, leaving dark reflections like spilled wine across the water's crystal surface, a fourth house was emerging from a new foundation.

Of the three current manors, TJ Donway swore this one would be the largest yet; the foundation alluding to a future dozen-car garage and a pit for a pool only the lake could rival. He wasn't sure of the number of rooms a space that large could contain, but he could discern, even through the distorted panoramic view across the water, his home could fit inside the new manor's foundation at least three times over. The borders of the future house butted up to the last inches of stable land against the water, threatening to spill over and fall right in. Wealth gave people all sorts of new ways to defy gravity.

TJ lived alone, having inherited his late parents' home thirty years ago, and saw no reason to move anywhere else. This icebox home was the perfect size for him, and it was small enough to feel cozy without becoming claustrophobic and large enough to feel like he could take space from himself when he changed rooms.

TJ's life was simple for the most part, and he wanted to keep it that way. On Sundays, he watched football on his outdated television, squinting to see the ball as it raced across the fuzzy field. He would heat a ready-made meal in the microwave and balance the hot black tray across his lap in front of the TV. When the weather permitted, TJ would open the windows of the two-bedroom house, letting the wind off the lake clear the stale air before pulling the windows back down and soaking up the outside welcomed in.

He liked the ease of living on the lake. Life made sense when he was here. He could be mindful of his thoughts without interruption. The lake was steady and always consistent, one of the few foundational parts of his life that had always been the same.

TJ had one sister, Amber, who lived with her husband Malcolm near the ocean, a few hours away. She'd invited him to their beach bungalow several times, but TJ didn't like the ocean. He'd always preferred the lake, with its stillness and steady rhythms. The lake had a predictability you couldn't get from the ocean, with its often violent tides and unforgiving attitude.

In the few times TJ had been to the ocean, the water had enveloped him, the noise, the vastness, cascading over the top of his head and taking him all the way into it.

There was no graceful way to be with the ocean.

When it came to the lake, TJ knew the right time to climb out to the dock and fish. He knew when to close the shutters just as large storms rolled in from the south and could count on when pleasant weather would bring college students bustling to the cold water in the hotter months of summer.

TJ had never swam in the lake, but he didn't feel like he had to. He could understand it without ever stepping down and being entirely within it. TJ knew it instinctively, how you know your arms and legs or the flavors on your favorite homemade dish. It was how you knew the embrace of a warm bed all your own.

TJ believed the lake must have some kind of ancient past as a gathering place for old-world civilizations, dependent on its water to survive.

He had made kin of the lake and had no intention of leaving.

That said, the rising manors on the other side of the water changed the lake in a way TJ hadn't seen before. Closing his eyes, he could imagine the vastness of looking across the water into a dense forest on the other side just a decade back. The lake had felt like a portal, a tunnel to something completely wild for those that dared to cross. When the day collapsed into the night and all the light with it, the lake looked back at him with an intense fullness that rivaled a new moon sky.

Now, the three manors poured light from the back decks of their yards into the lake all night long, shining spotlights on the black velvet water. It gave the lake a distinctly prison-like appearance, floodlights sculpting out defined shapes in the water, calling out all movement and making it discernible to the human eye. TJ had never understood why the lights were positioned to beam down into the water. He didn't know what could be worth looking for at the bottom.

The construction noise outside continued to get louder, even from across the water. TJ stepped back inside, closing the door behind him.

He returned to the tomato sandwich he'd left stranded and half-eaten on the kitchen counter. The mayo had grown warm between the thick slices of white bread as it soaked in the afternoon sunlight, giving it the distinctive taste of summer. Even with the door closed, TJ could still hear the rattling of construction and shoved two tomato-stained fingers into his ears.

Why do they have to be so damn loud? He wondered, taking his fingers out of his ears and wiping off the tomato juice with a paper towel.

The rattling continued to intensify, almost as if coming from inside TJ's home. TJ huffed, prepared to walk back onto his back porch and scream at the machinery across the water; before he realized this time, the noise was a stern knocking on his front door.

Discarding the final bite of his sandwich to the trash, TJ opened the door without peering through the broken peephole to find Amber grinning on his porch.

"Hi!" Amber waved as TJ brushed the stray crumbs off his dark pants.

"What are you doing here?" TJ asked.

Amber had shown up unannounced before, but never this enthusiastically and *only* when there was something to announce. She'd appeared at the door to tell him she was getting married or when she and Malcolm were leaving for Paris to celebrate their wedding anniversary. It was always for some kind of announcement.

Amber's life was only complete if she had a force of constant stimulation, a new experience, a new frontier. When their parents had died, it hadn't even been a question as to which one of them would get to keep the house.

"I'd rather kill myself than live where I grew up." Amber frowned, tapping her nails on the kitchen counter. The two stood together, surrounded by a lifetime of their parent's memories, sorting items for donation and the dumpster. They'd been there for hours, TJ hesitant about throwing out too many family heirlooms, while Amber quickly discarded anything she didn't recognize into one of the many large black trash bags.

"Besides," Amber continued, "do you have anywhere else to go?"

Today, TJ thought Amber's face might rip open from how broadly she was smiling; her hands clasped tightly together as if to hold her body in place to control the enthusiasm.

"Did you not see my text?" Amber blinked, her smile unwavering.

"No, I didn't," TJ thought of his discarded cell phone, perpetually on the charger in his bedroom, given how little he used it.

"Well, Malcolm's company is moving up north and inland..." Amber shuffled between her two feet, biting down hard on her bottom lip.

"And..?"

Amber huffed. "*And,* we're trying to get rid of a couple of things before we go, and I had the idea that there was something that might be of more use to you than it would be to us since we're going to be so far away from the water."

TJ narrowed his gaze. "What do you-"

Stepping back from the porch, Amber opened her arms wide and gestured behind her. Malcolm's truck was parked just down the street, and hitched to the back of it was a boat.

"Ta-da!" Amber laughed, clasping her hands together and looking back at TJ. "What do you think?"

TJ stepped off the porch, taking in the size of the vessel. The boat was pristine white, detailed with striking blue on both sides. It looked almost brand new. Even from behind Malcolm's truck, the boat nearly cleared the top of the house. It was immense on his small street, casting a shadow nearly as long as the pine trees.

"Amber, I can't take this from you."

Amber laughed.

"I wasn't asking if you *wanted* it. I'm giving it to you."

"I-" TJ stammered. He'd never been on a boat before or even seen one this nice.

"This must have cost a fortune. Can't you just sell it?"

Amber shook her head, her smile resolute. "I don't want to sell it. I want you to have it. Take it out on the lake. That would mean more to me than the money."

Looking between Amber and the boat, TJ froze in place. The boat was spectacular, but part of him felt like using it would somehow betray his relationship with the lake.

For so long, he'd relied purely on *his* understanding of the lake, what it said, what it meant; a boat could change that completely. It would be a new layer of connectivity with the lake, gliding across the water instead of looking across it. He would understand its depth in ways he'd never been able to, knowing what the manor's floodlights were doing, looking down and into the darkest parts of the water.

"I just don't know," TJ's arms hung limply at his sides. "It just... Doesn't feel like it's *me*."

"Come on, come look at it." Amber gestured to him, leading him back towards the boat.

The boat was even more magnificent up close, the detailed blue paint catching the glimmers of sunlight coming down through the trees, sparkling against the dark pavement.

"Don't think giving this to you is an easy choice," Amber continued. "This was an anniversary present from Malcolm's parents last year, and I do *hate* parting with it... I just... I don't know. I think it would be good for you to have something you can take on to the lake for once. Like mom and dad did, you know?"

TJ remembered their parent's boat. It was a small speedboat with a tiny engine strapped to the back of it. Only two people could fit on it at a time, or you risked the whole thing tumbling over. Algae was growing on both sides of it. The green paint faded from years spent in the sunlight. TJ had always been too scared to travel with his father out onto the water. Still, he remembered a young Amber screaming and clapping her hands in delight as their father drifted back and forth across the lake, making figure-eights that would cause waves to lap up against the side of the dock, splashing TJ's shorts.

"Mom and Dad could fit five of their boats onto this thing," TJ replied, reaching up and running his hand along the smooth side of the boat. "Maybe six."

Amber laughed. "Sure, but they'd be happy knowing you were going out on the water."

TJ stood behind the boat, inspecting the small deck and the curled cursive letters floating just above it: *The Grand Explorer*, it read.

"I know it's not the most creative name." Amber frowned. "But it's better than some sex pun. You should see how many people do that down on the coast."

Looking up at the boat, TJ reached up and ran his fingers over the letters. Maybe it would feel nice to glide on top of the water like his dad had, experiencing the lake in full, not just in part. TJ rested his hand down on the side of the boat, feeling the warm paint under his fingertips.

"Why's Malcolm's company moving?"

Amber ran her hand over the top of her hair. TJ could hear the wind.

"They're... *refocusing.* In light of some recent events, they're having the team move inwards and away from the coast."

TJ frowned, taking his hand off the back of the boat. "What kind of *events* are you talking about?"

Amber hesitated. "We've had advisories not to swim or visit the ocean in the last few weeks that... the public hasn't been given yet, and they're just trying to get ahead of the problem."

"By... Not telling anybody about it?"

"No," Amber frowned. "It's not like that. There's no reason to send people into... some kind of panic. Besides, they haven't been able to confirm anything with certainty yet."

TJ recalled his few memories of Malcolm, a tall and stern man who looked as if it had to be carved into his face when he smiled. He always seemed a bit ingenuine, at least to TJ, who had always suspected Amber had married him for the kind of life he could *provide* her, not a life *with* him. Malcolm had always worked for major companies, well off for his entire career. But Malcolm's job was always unclear to TJ. Anything he learned or heard Malcolm had discovered or helped the company champion felt like he was pulling magic numbers out of his hat, making up some kind of data to make them look good. His job didn't feel like a real one to TJ, and when Amber spoke fondly of his work, TJ always felt a pit forming in the center of his stomach.

"Isn't his company part of the reason why the water's been getting worse?"

"I mean..." Amber sighed, flustered. "It's not like it's been intentional, just... an accident. And besides, most of the manufacturing isn't done at that location, so there's no way that they could pinpoint anything-"

Amber cut herself off, pressing her lips closed together. "I think you're making a bigger deal out of this than it needs to be."

TJ frowned. "Hm."

The wind rustled through the pine trees, their shadows on the ground shifting underneath TJ's feet. The boat's shadow remained perfectly still, unwavering.

"Come on, TJ." Amber stepped up to him. "It's not *that* bad. Besides, Malcolm's working on the pollution monitoring team right now. Their ESG scores are through the roof this season, the company's making great progress if you check out their numbers-"

"But what's wrong with the water?"

Amber pressed her lips together. Her tell. "I- I don't know."

Several birds echoed above them from the pine trees.

"Yes, you do."

TJ stepped back from the boat, its presence suddenly becoming less impressive and more intimidating the longer he looked at it. It seemed menacing, the way it towered over the other small, older houses on the street. The vessel had become the captain of a community it didn't belong to.

"You know, you never even visited us out there," Amber huffed. "No matter how many times I invited you, you had no interest in seeing mine and Malcolm's life all because of the ocean or what he does for work or whatever keeps you rooted in this damn old house."

Amber folded her arms across her chest.

"You know, you live this little life here with your head buried in the sand, ignoring everyone and everything around you. Well, guess what, TJ, the world's changing, and the shit you think you understand or have some kind of insight on, you don't."

Amber grit her teeth. "But you're just too *fucking* stubborn."

The wind blew harder than before, whipping through the

trees like a choir singing out through the silence. TJ could hear the construction noise across the lake and the water lapping against the shore as the wind carried it forward.

"I don't want the boat," TJ said firmly, stepping away from Amber and turning back toward his house.

The wind continued parting space through the trees, bending their tops together in a thick green canopy and blocking some midday sun. The boat's glimmer grew dull in the sudden shade, making it small.

"Come on, TJ; I wasn't- I'm sorry, I *want* to give it to you." Amber chased after TJ, following him back towards the house.

"I don't want it, Amber."

"Please, it would be so good for you-"

"You don't know what's good for me the same way you don't know that not telling people where they're living might be *toxic* while you run for the hills is *fucked* up. I don't want any part of it."

Amber shakes her head. "You just-"

"No, Amber, I *do* get it. Trust me."

TJ stepped towards the house, the wind continuing to whip new shadows across the street with every change in intensity. He could feel his heartbeat pounding in his ears.

Amber dropped her folded arms, defeated at her sides, and looked on at TJ. "Fine."

Stepping onto the porch, TJ watched Amber walk back toward Malcolm's tall truck. She pulled her bleached hair back into a ponytail.

TJ could almost imagine her as a kid, hair still dark like his, bouncing wildly down her back after their dad on the dock. She went blonde after her wedding and hadn't gone back. They hardly looked related anymore.

"Didn't Malcolm's father used to work at the same company he's at now?" TJ shouted across to Amber just as she started to open the driver's side door. "Isn't that what money bought the boat?"

Amber looked at him from beside the truck, pressing her lips tight together. She opened her mouth briefly, as if fighting to say something else, but shut it. Amber climbed inside the truck and slammed the door before revving the engine.

TJ stood on the front porch, leaning against the doorframe, watching as Amber sped forward. The boat hitched behind her and turned quickly as she rushed back down the hill, spilling ocean water into the road in a stream behind the truck.

The wind picked up again, the trees parted, and sunlight streamed toward the water.

Walking inside, TJ stepped through the house and opened the backdoor to the dock, breathing in the air from the water. The construction noise had grown quiet; the loudest sound returned to the lapping of the lake against the beams of the old dock.

TJ looked out across the lake, sunlight catching on the tops of the small waves moving through it, and kicked off his boots. He looked at his bare feet, feeling like a kid again, standing on the dock but too afraid to go in.

Too scared of knowing.

Or maybe, just too stubborn to find out.

TJ took a deep breath and shimmied between the two lower beams at the back of the dock, took a deep breath, and turned around to lower his legs into the water.

The water flowed around his feet, and small swarms of tadpoles gathered across the tops of his toes before disappearing into the darker parts of the water. TJ took another two steps into the water, looking at the distant manors. Their looming presence was all the more noticeable from the height of the lake bed, three peering castles with many eyes casting down towards the water.

Nearing the center of the lake, TJ looked back toward his house, which had become a freckle on the face of the lakeshore. TJ kept walking, the water beginning to rise towards his calves and thighs, but it rose no further.

TJ frowned.

This didn't seem right. There was no way he'd reached the lake's center, and it was only this deep.

TJ trekked onward.

It has to get deeper. There's no way it's just this deep. No way.

The manors grew taller and taller in front of TJ, his home nearly disappearing as he continued to trek forward, but the water still rose no further than his thigh.

A small fish bumped into TJ's leg and sent him looking down and around the lake bed. For the first time, he saw it all clearly in a way no amount of time spent on the dock would ever show him: the falling water level, the erosion once concealed by standing at the top of the dock.

There was dried sand a few feet below the grass at the rim of the lake and dead lake plants scattering the shoreline like discarded toys, no longer usable.

How could it have looked so deep for so long?

TJ looked down at the water; clouds made way for the returning midday sun. The lake filled with light, returning the whole space to its original marsh brown color.

The only place still dark and unknown was below the three manors. Their long shadows cast dark nightlike colors onto the rest of the water, making it look miles deep below.

Taking another step forward, TJ charged towards the shadow of the mansions, letting the darkness envelop him the same way the ocean had all those years ago. The heat of the summer disappeared from his shoulders as he stepped into the shadow, but there was no all-encompassing water pouring over his head, no roar in his ears as he neared the darkest part of the water underneath the manors; encapsulated without sinking into a wave.

He was still in the water, only up to his thighs.

THROUGH NEIGHBORING WINDOWS

To not miss a moment of the night's award show, I decided to watch through my neighbor's window.

With my paws stained blue by discarded Halloween candy, I plunged my hand back into the bag in search of another blue raspberry sucker, shuffling between green apple and cherry until I found one. The candy was sickly sweet on the top of my tongue, and I rolled it back and forth across every cratered corner of my mouth, coating the whole thing in sweetness.

My father never liked when I got into his hidden bags of candy. They were always tucked in the darkest parts of the pantry, with his fluffy pastries concealed in boxes I couldn't open. The candy was easy to get to, one swift cut of claw through the plastic, and the sweets were mine for the taking.

Sitting here with my legs curled against the window frame and wrapped around the candy bag was my favorite past-time. The neighbor's TV casted pink, purple, and twinkling blue advertisements through their window, across the yard, and into my room. I couldn't count how many times I'd sat here, just a stone's throw from their couch and corner chairs, looking on fixated as if I was watching side by side with them too.

From this distance, I could barely distinguish the names and phrases stretched across the broad canopies of colored advertisements or the names of winning actors and actresses stretched underneath the award show pageantry. I could not read any of it; the only marker between the program and the commercials was watching my room transform with every new hue flashing between the different scenes and stories.

I liked watching TV like this; not having one of my own made it feel all the more remarkable when the family next door let theirs run late. It was perfect entertainment after I'd run out of rudimentary ways to occupy myself. How long could I really throw my unicorn toy against the wall without it getting old?

You could always count on a celebrity to do something interesting; their expensive skin and carved expressions filled the space between advertisements for cardiovascular health and evening news shorts about a serial rapist or a billionaire's latest cover-up on the toxic chemicals their company was leaking into the ocean. Entertainment was the perfect pacifier, one even I couldn't resist.

Suddenly, from the corner of my eyes fixed on the screen, I spotted a quiet lizard making haste away from the backdoor.

He was little, unassuming, body canvassed by dark white and beige stripes and staring down at me from his new corner of the world.

I hadn't seen him before, at least not in this room. Or perhaps, I'd only imagined having other interactions with this small fellow, black eyes fixated with familiarity.

Still, he must be nervous. Didn't he know better than to come into a room of predators?

I wiped my paws clean before I could assess the situation. They were stained and sweet, and I folded them neatly at my sides as I peered up towards the lizard's body. He tilted his head, wiggled his front feet, and bolted for the room's far corner.

Swiftly as I could muster, I managed to grab the tiny

creature up by his tail in my mouth and rested him in front of me. He was frozen in place.

Mhmm…. I looked him over. *This might be a pleasant snack.*

The lizard sank deeper into the tile, his beaded eyes wide.

Perhaps, a truce this time.

Slowly but surely, I picked him back up into my mouth and carried him to the backdoor.

We walked together towards the grassy backyard, where my toes sank into the wet dirt as I set him down. He didn't move.

"Come on, you know this place," I nudged as if all the outside must possibly look the same to something fractionally my size. "You don't have to be scared anymore."

We were in his home now, and I was just a visitor, passing through nature the same way I'd weave between each of the house's different rooms. I was a guest, not obliged to live out here and be in the same spaces as he did. My home was within the walls I occupied, within the corners of my space. His home had no boundaries; the corners extended as far as he was willing to go.

I could hear the neighbor's TV even outside and see the multicolor glow reach across the wet grass. The light tinted it in different shades the same way it did in my room, only bending with the texture of the grass into deeper, elongated shadows.

The lizard turned his small head back and up to me, blinking in what I read as disbelief. Maybe contentment, maybe indifference. He frowned with his small mouth, flaring his thin nostrils open and closed against the night air.

Laughter radiated from across the neighbor's house and into the outside. After turning back to the source of the noise and then forward again, the lizard bolted away and disappeared, sinking somewhere into the technicolor grass and towards the trees.

I found myself a bit jealous of his freedom, his ability to wander within different spaces without ever having to be bound to one.

Maybe I should have eaten him.

I would not see the lizard again in the guest bedroom, share water with him in the kitchen, or find his peering black eyes looking down at me from the ceiling as I watched the neighbor's TV. I supposed the lizard was also a neighbor, but our shared property line was blurred by trees, concave brush bushes, and fallen wood; neither of us bothered to learn who the fence belonged to, where it started, and where it stopped. There was also no TV to watch.

The light disappeared as the neighbor's TV turned off; I noticed the absence immediately, a bad habit ingrained by my domesticity and the need for something to pay attention to. The grass had returned to its natural shade of dark green, illuminated only by the light of my back porch.

I looked down at my paws, sticking to the wet grass and mud, leaving four indentations like tidal pools in the ground. I ran my nose along the outline, feeling where the weight of my paws displaced the dirt, the borders and plant fibers tickling against my whiskers.

Turning back towards the house, I looked down at my paws, caked with thick dirt and stained not blue but dark brown.

I licked each one clean.

JAZZ NIGHT AT MELBAS

Out of all the days of the week, Thursdays were Martin's favorite. Catrina had the kids, staff meetings always ran short, and it was Jazz Night at Melbas.

Martin spent most of Thursday longingly looking at his saxophone tucked in the corner of his locker room office, counting down the minutes until school was out and he could enter the city.

This Thursday had moved particularly slow, the cranked AC pumping into the office, making Martin's fingers curl around his keyboard. The cold exhausted him, but there was no way for him to turn it down. The switch was hidden somewhere in the maintenance office he couldn't reach.

Martin had only written a single referral today and had overseen the tenth-grade girl's mile test. Even by high school gym coach standards, today was a particular type of boring.

Martin's eye flickered back and forth to the clock on the wall, second hand taunting him in a steady rhythm. He internalized the pulse, feeling each bouncing click like a metronome driving the song in a forward march. He found himself tapping his fingers against his keyboard in time with the rhythm, marching his fingers down and across the keys.

Having always loved music, a gym coach had never been Martin's first choice in a career. He diddled around over the years back and forth between different professions, office jobs, and restaurant management, but none of them quite allowed the freedom like teaching to attend Jazz Night at Melbas.

Melbas was a traditional dive jazz bar in many ways but unconventional in just as many others. Sandwiched between an abandoned department store and the county clerk's office, Melbas had historically been a thorn in the side of the modernizing city.

Somehow, this made Melbas all the more special to Martin. The bar attracted a sort of crowd the city wasn't particularly fond of, musicians in mixed pattern play clothes, a back porch that was ripe with the smell of cigarettes and stale beer, a parking lot in a grass coat that butted up against the county clerk's property line. No one that worked in the clerk's office enjoyed the presence of Melba's next door, though Martin had once tried to get a job in the building to be closer to it.

Martin loved Melbas' because it was a community gathering place where people and their identities existed uniquely. No one knew about the roles anyone played outside Melba's front doors. Inside, people were artists, unphased by the day-to-day realities and trials outside of them. Leaning against worn-out furniture and against a wall that had grown textured from thumbtacks and pen scratches, Martin had found a community of people where he was Martin the Musician. Not Martin the Gym Coach or Martin the Father or Martin the Husband. He appreciated the alternative side of his persona that only Melbas could give him.

Outside of Melbas, Martin the Musician didn't exist.

The day dragged on, unaware of Martin's frustration, or at least, unsympathetic to it. He glanced at the small watch on his wrist, the clock on the wall, and the digital clock in the far right corner of his computer screen. Martin waited anxiously as his contracted hours quickly drew to a close, rising from his desk in anticipation.

There was a knock on his office door, and the school dean, Emmett, stepped in through the door. Martin sat back down, trying his best to look busy.

"Hey, just wanted to see if you have any more problems with the Wilde sister."

Martin shook his head. "No, Rose was much better today."

Emmett nodded. "Good. We don't need her causing any more issues. It's already been chaotic enough dealing with her parents."

Emmett wasn't an exceptionally compassionate dean, but he got the job done. Martin had always been alarmed by how hollowed out he looked, and he could never tell if it was from age or bitterness.

"Well," Emmett huffed. "Any plans tonight?"

Martin swallowed, fiddling with the pencil on his desk. "Nah, just a quiet night."

"Me neither. Nothing better than that," Emmett managed a smile. Martin nodded towards him as he closed the door. "Have a goodnight."

"You too."

Martin took a deep breath and turned back to his computer. He scrolled through the news and saw another story about the chemical leak in the ocean, sending much of the public packing from the shoreline, and about the death of a former student, Elliot Wilde, in a car accident, whose younger sister Rose had been acting up the past few days.

Martin chewed on the inside of his cheek. The world was getting so bleak, faster than he'd ever seen it happen before. Everything was changing, and the old world was growing closer to dying off entirely. That was why he clung so tightly to Melbas and his jazz nights. Where the music was uncertain, but the gathering was not.

He shut down his computer and filed away the last of his

things, the anticipation and anxiety buzzing in his hands.

Martin rushed to clean the school gymnasium floors, his nose filling with the smell of the linoleum cleaner and laundry detergent from the industrial washing machines for the gym clothes. His head was already buzzing with melodies to play tonight, riffing off conventional jazz standards and creating extra complexity on the saxophone to fill the space left by the other players. He was excited to collaborate, hear about what other people had been listening to, and talk about something other than why you couldn't hit your friend with your lunchbox or that a twenty-minute mile was unacceptable for a fifteen-year-old.

Martin swung his mop around his back, running into a slide as he dragged it out across the gym floor, covering the school seal in a layer of shiny fluid. The cleaner reflected the harsh gymnasium lighting up to the ceiling like a stage light. Martin grinned, shuffling his feet around in a brief dance in the empty gymnasium, melodies fluttering throughout his head. He emptied the remaining water in the bucket down one of the drains in the shower, flicked the overhead lights off, and rushed for the door, locking it closed.

He was finally free.

The change of clothes Martin left in the car had grown warm through the day, the fabric easing the tension the cold had left in his hands. Martin grabbed the hem of his polo shirt and exchanged it for a favorite t-shirt and casual pants. Looking around, he crawled into the back of his car and quickly changed, kicking his feet against the window and sliding into a pair of jeans. He hadn't been outside since this morning, but the daylight was exceptional. He couldn't remember the last time it had been this nice out.

Martin was so excited he could hear his heartbeat pulsing in his ears as he slipped the key into the ignition and sped out of the school parking lot towards the city.

Rush hour greeted him with its usual snail's pace crawl. Though the cars moved slowly along the vast and curving highway, this was a welcome change in Martin's traditional commute through the suburbs. City roads were different; they buzzed with personality, where the suburbs had traffic, the city retained its purpose.

People were going somewhere, not retreating.

The city's lights speckled in the distance, growing brighter as he inched closer. Shining skyscrapers hosted hoverboard platforms for the billionaires, landing helicopters and planes for their second and third wives returning from islands off the coast. The skyscraper needles reached toward the clouds as if trying to pierce directly into space, and with every new building, the distance to the stratosphere grew shorter. There were already several new buildings Martin didn't recognize, even from just last week.

Huddled around these mammoth skyscrapers were the remains of the old city, shorter-several-story buildings and houses dotted along the borders, dwarfed by their younger brothers. Few businesses remained of this era of the city.

Most had lost court battles in city "beautification" programs, failing to prove their use in a way that enabled profits and being fated to bulldozers and new foundations provided by private industry for the few, now inaccessible to the masses.

Miraculously, Melbas had continued to avoid the same fate as its neighbors. Maybe it was because it was a refuge for cheating billionaires to sink away and form their own alternative identities, making it valuable enough not to lose.

Still, with every new skyscraper installation, Melbas looked more like a relic from centuries ago.

Martin pulled off the exit, paid the $45 bridge toll, his least favorite part about coming into the city, and drove to Melbas, tapping excitedly on the top of his steering wheel.

He felt the car bounce from the freshly paved asphalt to the textured older roads on the outskirts. Resurfacing projects were reserved for more valuable areas of the city.

Reaching a stoplight, Martin flicked down the mirror and checked his hair, combing it back with his fingers and rubbing the sleep from his expression. He examined his face, the shadows migrating from his dark eyes on top of his cheeks. He was getting older, and he could feel it. A teacher's salary didn't allow him the extra income to afford world-class treatments to fix his skin and puff his face back up with chemical youth. Usually, it bothered him to see himself in the mirror like this, but at this moment, he didn't mind. The age felt like a badge of honor when he played music; it came with a knowingness younger players didn't have yet.

The day was fading into the night, but Martin felt more awake than he had the whole day as he pulled into Melba's grassy parking lot.

"Martin!"

Someone called his name in the distance, and he spotted Diego holding his unicycle and dropping a cigarette butt. Diego rushed towards the driver's side door; Martin grinned as he got closer. Diego was also Melbas regular.

"Hey!" Martin waved, rolling the window down.

"So glad you made it," Diego grinned, clamping his hand on his shoulder cheerfully.

Martin laughed as if there was anywhere else he could be on a Thursday. Martin hadn't missed a Thursday Jazz Night at Melbas since his son was born. He would be fifteen this year.

Martin parked the car and stepped around to the back to grab his saxophone.

"How are you doing, man?" Diego asked, leaning his hip on the car door.

Martin set his saxophone down behind his car.

"I've had this melody stuck in my head all day that I can't wait to try out tonight," Martin slammed the truck door closed, lifting the saxophone off the grass.

"It's gonna be a good one. I can feel it. It's been playing in my head like it's already writing itself into a story."

"Ahh! That's what I like to fucking hear!" Diego honked the miniature clown horn he kept on his keychain in approval.

Diego's dark hair was matted and messy, his face tinted green on both cheeks and sparkling yellow glitter across the tops of his eyelids. He was a city person, more exposed to

the eccentric and changing styles of the wealthy than Martin
was. The rich had begun painting their faces more elaborately,
drawing out their features in clustered and non-traditional
colors. Diego, who was nowhere near as wealthy, had his own
interpretation of their outlandish style, which made him look
a bit like a court jester. The clown horn didn't help.

"What about you?" Martin asked, the two men walking
together towards Melbas' front porch, stepping aside for the
straggling county clerk employees looking disapprovingly at
the two men, specifically Diego, who was shirtless.

"Oh, you know, just practicing, trying to find out the way
to get my thoughts on paper," Diego, a writer and birthday
party performer, had been writing his debut screenplay for
over a decade and had teased that this year would be the one
that he finished it.

"I happened to run into some big wig the other day who
said he worked for the studios. I got his TikTok username,
and he told me to message him when the script was ready, and
he might be able to pull some strings. This could be my big
break!" Diego squeezed the horn on the unicycle again with
such joy that it deflated entirely before refilling with a muffled
"phwww."

"Great news!" Martin patted Diego on the back, reaching
for Melba's front door and stepping inside. "I hope that works
out."

Diego laughed. "I do too. The last time I have to perform
at a screaming billionaire's kid's birthday party, I'll be the
happiest man alive. To finally be doing what I want, that's a
dream."

Martin nodded, thinking about the glowing linoleum
lights on the clean gym floor. The memory distorted itself, the
gym turning into a stage, and he was playing saxophone right
in the center of it.

Was there a world like that left for him? A world to dream of?

The front door of Melbas had a gold plaque that had been
there for as long as Martin could remember; a shining "M."
He reached up to the door and ran his fingers across the "M,"

and warmth spread across his chest.

He was home.

The lighting was dim as the pair walked inside. Three people on the small stage up front were setting up the jazz drum kit for the jam tonight.

It was quieter than usual for a Thursday. A handful of regulars waved to Martin as he came in, all nursing cups of coffee. A young girl sketched in the corner. A couple held hands across the table, speaking quietly.

"Where is everybody?" Martin asked Diego, setting down his saxophone case.

"Dunno, maybe that new place down the road."

Martin frowned. "What new place?"

Diego tapped his forehead. "I forgot to tell you! There's some new fancy fucking coffee shop down the road. They're hosting a Thursday Jazz Night too. It's sponsored by one of those rich tech companies. Coffee made in a lab, no employees, and you can apply for a credit card at the front counter."

Martin frowned. That didn't sound the least bit nice. "They're hosting a jazz night?"

Diego nodded, "Lame, I know, but it's in a nicer part of the city. In the base of one of the super skyscrapers, kind of impressive."

Pulling out one of the worn wooden chairs, Martin sat down, tapping on the table. "I mean, it can't have drawn too many people away. Melbas is Melbas."

Diego sat beside him, shrugging, resting the unicycle on the table. "Maybe, but Melbas doesn't let you pay for your coffee with your watch and donate 1% to a charity of your choice."

Martin frowned. "Have you been?"

"Course. I wanted to see what all the hype was about. Owner says he's got big plans for the place, trying to champion some Community Center as a Service thing, CCaaS or whatever, and sell the idea around the city."

"That sounds absurd."

"People are eating it up."

Scattered people began shuffling in and out of Melbas, several taking coffee and pastries to go, others plugging headphones in and opening up laptops to work. Martin tapped his fingers anxiously on the top of his saxophone case, watching the door for any others that may come in holding instruments, checking his watch. His stomach felt uneasy, the tension returning to his fingers.

Was everyone over there?

Martin ordered tea for himself and Diego, draining almost half of it before standing up.

"Take me to the stupid billionaire coffee shop."

"What-"

"If everybody's there, I want to see what all the fuss is about."

"Okay, if you're sure."

Martin rushed out the front door, putting his saxophone in the car's trunk with Diego's unicycle, and backed his car out of Melbas' grass lot. Diego pointed directions and turned into the newer section of the city.

Bright, flashy buildings sprang from the ground in technicolor displays, glass walls towering above the car and reflecting their light on the top of Martin's car like the linoleum on the gym floor. Martin stared up at the buildings, realizing he'd never been this close to anything remotely this tall.

"There it is," Diego called, pointing to one of the tallest buildings in all of downtown. There was no parking lot, so Martin rushed for an open street parking spot and paid the $30 for 30 minutes parking fee, grimaced, and slid his card into the machine. He'd spent $75 to be in the city, more than he made in a whole day of work.

Walking in this part of the city, as modern, clean, and high-tech as it was, felt like walking in the suburbs. Everything was manicured and tailored to fit a particular style, the sidewalks had just enough space for several pedestrians, and manicured greenery provided an ambiance without intruding too much. It felt like the highly controlled version of cities Martin had become familiar with in the last decade, lacking character. These buildings had the same energy as the suburbs: bland and sterile.

The two men made it to the front doors of the cafe, placed their hands against the glass handle, and pulled it open. The air inside was perfectly cool, the room's scent rich with coffee beans and fresh pastries.

Martin looked behind the bar to see no employees, just two robotic arms shaking and mixing coffee drinks and two matching kiosks, one for drinks and the other for credit card applications.

"This is... ridiculous." Martin frowned.

Sure, the place was cleaner and *smelled* better–hell, it definitely *looked* better than Melbas, but something felt so sterile here. It was like you were standing in a hospital and being asked to relax while your bones tensed up under the artificial sun.

"You gotta admit, it's kinda cool," Diego whispered. "The coffee's pretty good too, so I've heard."

"I don't care," Martin sighed. "Where's the authenticity? What's real about this place? Where's the *connection?*"

Diego looked around the room.

"Maybe in *The Connection Space...?*"

"What?"

Diego pointed up at a sign just near the back of the atrium that read "*The Connection Space,*" While peering around the corner, Martin heard the sound of jazz music and conversation down the hallway. Martin's jaw softened. The music was exceptionally beautiful, better than anything he'd ever heard before.

"Come on," Martin whispered.

Following his ear, Martin led Diego through the tight hallway into a white circular room with several chairs outlining a circle. In the middle were several controllers, playing different jazz progressions as people, some of whom Martin recognized from Melbas, watched and listened to the robots, jamming along. It sounded brilliant, but not a single human was playing.

"What is this?" Martin asked, feeling his chest tighten. "This is what they're calling a *jazz night*?"

A woman in the second row of the circle turned back to look at the two men. "Martin?" she asked.

"Octavia," Martin stepped towards her. Octavia was a brilliant jazz singer, and her scatting was some of the best in the Melbas community. She sat comfortably in one of the chairs, her arms resting gently in a pile on her lap. Octavia looked like she was nearly in a trance, nodding along to the sterile robot melodies.

"Why aren't you at Melbas?" Martin asked.

"Well, everyone seemed to be coming here tonight. I'd never been, and it's fun to try something new. The music has been quite good."

"But, it's just... robots? You can't tell me you think this is as good as Melbas' Jazz Night?" Martin felt the heat rise in his chest.

"Come on, don't you want to sing a little?"

Octavia shrugged. "It's nice just to listen."

The sharpness in Martin's stomach intensified.

The song of the robots continued to play on before ending in a crescendo and going quiet. The small circle audience clapped, faces painted in rainbow shades like Diego's, standing out like misplaced objects against the shallow white room.

There was a brief pause and the sound of gears and computer whirr before the next song began, the controllers lighting up with different instrumentation as the robots pressed on the keys.

"This is kinda cool." Diego sat beside Octavia, leaning back and watching the robots, eyes widening. Martin frowned.

"Come on," Diego whispered. "You have to admit the technology is amazing"

"I-" Martin was stunned. "This isn't a jam. This isn't what jazz nights are about. This is-"

Martin paused as the robot riffed on its imaginary

trumpet. Several audience members clapped.

"Frankly, I don't even know what this is, but I don't like it. Not at all."

Martin's heart pounded as he turned back down the hallway towards the coffee shop and pushed open the front doors. He tried to steady himself as he ignored Diego and Octavia calling back to him, begging him to stay and "just give it a chance."

His head was spinning, and he was angry, but more than that, he was hurt. Melbas was his community. Melbas was his solace away from the everyday world without music, a world without color. Every day spent in bland environments was worth it when he came to Melbas and felt like he was alive, not just living.

Would Melbas be taken away from him too?

Martin turned his car on and raced back toward Melbas, paying another $42 for spending thirty-one minutes in the coffee shop, but he didn't care. He would have paid anything to get out of there.

Displeased, Martin frowned at the new buildings with their flashing lights, the sounds of the helicopters racing above his head with the rich people, their expensive coffee and designer robots, and lifeless jazz nights. He hated how this part of the city made him feel like he shouldn't have left the suburbs at all.

Only moments after parking back in Melbas' grassy lot, Martin grabbed his saxophone from the trunk and stepped through Melbas' front door. The cafe was still quiet and dimly lit. The barista pulled an espresso shot for the stray man at the bar, and several college-aged girls studied over laptops and notecards in the back corner.

No one was on the stage for Jazz Night.

Martin stepped onto the stage slowly, laying down his saxophone case and gently unclicking each lock in perfect rhythm. The saxophone caught the dim light of Melbas as he pulled it from his case, the metal cool against his hands.

In the absence of other players, several chairs usually

positioned on stage for jazz night had been picked up and moved back to different spots around the cafe, leaving just two.

No one watched as Martin the Musician stepped up onto the stage.

Sitting down, Martin rested his saxophone on crossed legs, looking around at the small groups of people in Melbas. The espresso machine hissed, the sounds of bustling city traffic from the interstate just barely audible over the shuffling of feet and papers in spotted locations around the room.

Martin's brain was fuzzy. He could still smell the detergent from the gym; his nose scrunched up at the thought of still being there in that room where he was confined over and over again, daydreaming of being somewhere else. The noise of the school, the city, the robots, and their unfeeling jazz music all buzzed in his ears; he felt the rattling down and into his bones.

For a moment, he was twenty again, standing in the back of his college jazz class, begging to get chosen for the Fall Recital's Elite Players, a collection of the best in class. He watched as his director read off the list, pulling several of his friends, while he stood bowlegged, staring at a group of people that didn't include him until his director looked up and pointed across the room.

"Come on over, Martin," She grinned, gesturing for him to join them.

The classroom light was warm on his face, and his friends patted him on the back as he joined them. He'd been good enough, he'd been chosen, and there was a chance for him to do this. It was real.

He looked down at the creases and age on his hands, the canyons of time carving accented marks he would carry with him until he was dead; the only reflection that time was passing both around him and within him.

He'd waited all day to be here.

He'd waited his whole life.

Martin took a deep breath and began to play the melody that had been inside his head for hours, and for the first time all day, everything was quiet.

INDICATOR

Clustered under blinking, half-lit Christmas lights, Natalia completed the conjoined list of grocery items for the week, written in hurried handwriting next to her hopes and dreams for the new year.

Looking it over, the list didn't seem all that impressive.

Rallying each bullet point off her fingers, Natalia counts just eight items on each list, requests for produce and powdered milk mixed in between the desire to visit Brazil, find a new job, and find a way to make herself happy.

The colored Christmas lights change the color of the white paper clutched in her hand from red to green, to blue and back again, temporarily muting the hue of the pen's ink, making the reminder to buy goat cheese and her dream of moving into a two bedroom apartment glow in the same hue.

Downtown was particularly quiet for the 23rd of December, just a few days before the holiday, but Natalia had the street all to herself. Only the small clothing resale store where she worked and the gas station had their lights on.

Natalia pretended she was in a movie as she scribbled down the list, her ungloved fingers shaking around the pen. It was still warmer than usual for this time of year.

Beyond the occasional passing car or the sound of the wind, as it stirred between the buildings, it was as if all the world's attention was focused on her and this moment.

She didn't feel like that a lot, if ever. She wasn't a performer or particularly intelligent. She'd never played a sport or had a hobby she poured all her life's desire into. Natalia liked her job with her friends at the clothing store but didn't love it. Natalia had good grades, but she'd like to do better. Natalia would like to make a difference but didn't know how.

In most ways, Natalia felt ordinary, confined to the simplicities of living like all regular citizens were. It didn't make her unhappy. It wasn't even something she thought about all that often. In the rare moment when life felt indifferent, Natalia wished it didn't always have to be so ordinary and tried to believe that extraordinary things could still happen.

Natalia continued staring at the list and the subtle creases in the paper made by the pressure from her fingers, a reminder that both lists were somehow equally tangible; dreams as much as groceries.

It was surreal to see all of it written out on the paper, in semi-actualized manifestations of the thoughts she'd rattle off during her lunch break or on the commute home. Between jumping to her next train and searching for her car at the back of the parking lot, days spent with her friends at their childhood lake that was drying up, Natalia felt like she was always dreaming of the future.

Yet, the thoughts of the future usually didn't make it any further than sitting in her car and turning on the radio, the music pushing her reflections far from her head.

The dried ink on the paper made the dreams seem real and, at least, somewhat *less* like maladaptive daydreams. She didn't know what had compelled her to write them down tonight; there was no trigger, sudden realization, inspirational quote, or deadline. She just knew, as she wrote out the ingredients for stir fry and a reminder to pick up dog food, it was time.

Natalia looked out at the streetlights, counting each bulb that had gone out and left short shadows scattered across the street. There were eight evenly spaced along the row, so coordinated it almost looked planned.

As the snow fell within the boundaries of the light's absence, it disappeared and lost its shimmer, silent and invisible but still piled on the ground.

Looking down at the list again, Natalia grinned just as the rest of the scattered Christmas lights took their final bow, blinked once more, and went black.

The list in her hands returned to a creamy shade of white, black ink bold against the background, her dreams and groceries front and center.

Natalia shivered and folded the paper into a tight square before stepping out from underneath the awning and down the road, walking in and out of the light.

MY ROOMMATE, ELLIOT

Seated criss-cross in front of an open refrigerator, Charlie wondered about the ethical considerations of whether or not you could eat your dead roommate's food.

Squared between the nearly empty water pitcher and a poorly rewrapped sandwich Charlie had attempted to eat for lunch was an entire plastic container of strawberries, washed and sliced by Elliot just a few days ago. Their skin was still perfectly red, and strawberry juice pooled at the bottom of the plastic container.

Charlie scooted closer to the shelves in the fridge, feeling the cold air against her face as she leaned in and pulled the container out.

The strawberries looked perfect, almost as if they had been bought today. This had been one of Elliot's many talents, his organization and ability to ensure every element of his life was planned out and cared for without requiring intervention.

Even in his passing, his strawberries persisted.

Elliot loved strawberries, though the harvest season had

dwindled over the years of climate change. For as long as she'd known him, Elliot had always made a big deal about going together to one of the local farms each year for the summer strawberry festival, filling two large blue baskets up to the brim with strawberries to bring home. It was one of the only activities they did together.

Elliot would use the strawberries more often than anyone Charlie knew, slicing them for sandwiches, tossing them into salads, baking them into pies, making his own rich salad dressing, anything you could add strawberries to; Elliot had done it.

Charlie had recommended he write a cookbook full of strawberry-based recipes.

"You could make a fortune off something like that," she'd told him. "*500 Ways to Use Strawberries, by Elliot Wilde*. Your name even sounds like a famous author."

Elliot had laughed and brushed it off. "Maybe someday, but it's not in the plan right now."

Charlie had only asked him once, what spawned the obsession with the fruit, but Elliot had never given her an honest answer, only citing their vitamin benefits or that he simply liked the flavor. The two of them had spent hours in the kitchen together, hunched over one cutting board, each taking a side to slice the strawberries from their stems into perfectly edible pieces, four hands growing stained with the red juice.

Elliot would bring a strawberry pie to their neighbor and another to his office when they met in person once a week when the smog wasn't as bad in the city, and it was safe to drive. Even when it wasn't safe to drive, Elliot always ensured Charlie's mother had access to fresh strawberries, whether or not it meant he was venturing into the heavy smog across the city, smog she'd later attribute to causing him to run the yellow light and swerve to miss a woman on a bike, crashing his truck to his death.

But that was the thing about Elliot. He was the kindest person Charlie had ever known, even if that meant putting himself second.

They'd met by chance, through a mutual friend at a college party, both strapped for cash and looking for a new place to live. They bonded over a shared love of terrible romance novels. They pretended to drink beer at the frat parties, secretly dumping their full cups out the open windows to let out the smell of cigarettes and marijuana.

Together, they'd sneak up to the roof of the crowded frat house, talking about how much they hated these parties but always ended up going anyway. It wasn't like there was much else to do. One night, they agreed to move in together above the echoing pulse of a club song neither of them knew by name, but both nodded along to.

Elliot came from a wealthy family, had a good job, and offered to pay the deposit for their two-bedroom apartment just off their college campus, the same place they'd now lived in for the last few years.

This was the same apartment where Elliot's stuff was now packed up in various corners around the space, boxes his family had requested, clothing to be donated, and several unclaimed momentos Charlie wasn't sure what to do with.

Charlie assumed the role of sorting Elliot's things simply because she was the closest in proximity to doing so. No one had asked her to pitch in, but after Elliot died, no one had come by to help. Slowly, Charlie had started separating things, answering the phone and telling relatives she'd sort everything and get something mailed back to them. Plenty of people had pieces of Elliot they'd like to remember, but Charlie was the only one ensuring they got them.

The fridge buzzed, but otherwise, the apartment was completely silent. For the first time in the years she'd been living there, Charlie felt overwhelmed by the space and the quiet. The sun was setting through the back window, the apartment slowly fading through the dusk with only the refrigerator light breaking through the shadowed space. Charlie's fingers danced along the top of the clear container of strawberries, her hand casting a shadow in the fridge light.

It was Thursday; Elliot would have had friends over tonight. Charlie would have just stepped out of her room, hearing the shuffling of feet from some of Elliot's friends making their way into the living room to hang out or play video games. She would step quietly into the kitchen to retrieve a bowl of granola and almond milk, her first meal of the day, and wave politely when she was acknowledged by the group before sinking back behind her door. She didn't ask to hang out with Elliot and his friends, she didn't think they were close like that, and she didn't want to intrude.

Now, she didn't bother with closing off her bedroom. After all, who was she asking for privacy from?

Charlie shifted around on the kitchen floor; her hips had grown uncomfortably thin over the past few weeks, the bones jutting into the tile with too little flesh in between.

Meals had become increasingly hard since Elliot died; he'd often been the keeper of making sure Charlie made herself something for dinner and got her to step away from her canvas for a few minutes to try a bite of the pasta he'd been cooking in the kitchen.

On days where she stayed up all through the night creating or quietly taking care of the virtual pets she'd had since she was a kid in an ancient computer game, if Elliot found her semi-passed out of the couch, he'd leave something small for her to eat before he started working. Charlie and Elliot had never talked about these situations directly. Charlie couldn't remember if she'd ever properly thanked him for any of them, only quietly putting the dishes in the washer after she ate whatever he'd left out for her.

That was the other thing that had changed since Elliot died: the apartment was filthy. Dirty dishes, half-empty paint bottles, and trash were dispersed indiscriminately all over the apartment. Charlie knew she should clean up, and it was making the place smell like old food and paint. But since Elliot was gone, there wasn't anyone coming over, no one to keep comfortable beside herself, which Charlie didn't typically care about doing. The trash gathering throughout the apartment had been more of a sign of life in this place than actual, living people had in weeks.

Elliot had always been the more social one of the two of them, always going out of his way to approach others. Charlie spent most of her time locked in her room, sleeping with her dark curtains pulled tightly over the windows or manically creating deep into the middle of the night.

That schedule didn't leave her much time to make connections like Elliot's, and Charlie was never really good with people. She'd always been impressed with the ease Elliot kept when interacting with strangers, often being approached in public for questions or greeted with a smile whenever they went anywhere. He was warm in all the ways that Charlie was cold, radiating energy outwards when Charlie felt she had none to spare.

Charlie felt her legs growing numb, so she stood up from the floor and let the fridge swing closed, leaving the strawberry container on the floor and walking into the living room towards the window.

Two half-painted canvases sat tucked in the corner, pieces Charlie had been working on just before Elliot died. They were commissioned pieces, the first two in a while, and the orders came in just in time. Charlie's bank account had been growing thin, and she needed to pay rent.

Since Elliot had died, the two canvases sat abandoned in the corner, dried in sections she'd started on but were otherwise incomplete, the color and white space butting up against each other in a stark divide.

Charlie had let the buyer, a pastor's wife looking for an updated family portrait, know the project would be delayed because of some personal challenges, but how long could you use grief as an excuse before it became a choice?

Charlie assumed she'd hear from them any day now to back out of the commission and leave her with two half-finished paintings and nothing else.

Elliot had been so excited when she told him about the commissions, clapping his hands and placing them on her shoulders, grinning.

"See! I told you it was only a matter of time, and you didn't believe me."

"It's just *one* commission-"

"Stop it." Elliot frowned. "Be excited! You can ruin anything if you *minimize* it, and what's the point of that?"

Charlie didn't know the point.

She knew she could finish the paintings; it wasn't like she'd forgotten how to paint, and she had everything she needed to complete them. But even standing this close to the canvases made her feel uneasy, and she couldn't pinpoint it.

She hadn't cried once since Elliot died, not when the police asked her to identify his body at the car accident, not when she had to use his cellphone to call his mom and sister Rose, not at the funeral when she told a room full of strangers what a good roommate he was.

And that was the word she'd always used; Elliot was her *roommate*.

Elliot had his circle of friends and a family Charlie had never met until he died. She and Elliot had existed in the same ecosystem through their shared environment, but she'd never referred to Elliot as anything *more* than her roommate. He was her friend, sure, but she never called him that. Elliot was always just *Elliot*, the guy she lived with, but now, he was just gone.

The people at Elliot's funeral were faces that Charlie didn't recognize. Their college friends had departed long ago and couldn't attend the funeral. She spotted a few familiar faces from Elliot's Thursday Night friend group, but they were only people she'd seen in passing trips to and from the kitchen, not people she knew.

The sea of strangers wiped tears from their noses, leaned on each other as Charlie spoke about an Elliot that made good food and always smiled, took her to get boba when her girlfriend broke up with her without warning, and offered her his streaming passwords. Elliot had asked a man she was seeing to leave their apartment after she discovered he'd been cheating on her.

She described an Elliot that never complained. An Elliot that she'd do anything to have back, even for a moment.

They'd clapped for Charlie as she finished speaking, unaware that behind the podium, she'd dug her fingernails down into the sides of her thigh, steadying herself in front of a room that had no idea who she was, terrified by the number of eyes on her.

She hadn't originally wanted to speak at the funeral, sitting quietly in the back, not having to approach the closed coffin concealing the body she'd already seen and identified while it was rough and battered; a moment she'd rather not relive.

In the end, when the open invitation was extended for people to speak, she stepped up to the podium and talked about her roommate Elliot.

Because he would have done the same for her.

"You spoke such kind words up there," Elliot's mother whispered to Charlie after she stepped down, slowly releasing her hand from her thigh. "Thank you for honoring him that way."

Charlie nodded, afraid that if she opened her mouth, the words wouldn't stop.

"We're building a new house on the lake. Please know you're welcome anytime. Elliot had nothing but good things to say about you."

Charlie looked into her eyes and realized they were the same deep, warm shade as Elliot's. His mother wrapped her arm up and around Rose. Charlie almost threw up, nodded a smile, and raced toward the back of the room.

She didn't feel like she'd said any of the right things up there because what did she *really* know about Elliot besides what he'd done for *her*?

What did she know about what or who he loved or what he wanted?

She only *knew* one thing about Elliot:

He loved strawberries.

What did that say about her?

The apartment had grown cold and dark, and Charlie turned away from the canvases and the window, feeling her way back to the kitchen. On her way out, she accidentally knocked her foot against the container of strawberries on the floor, sending it sliding deeper into the kitchen.

Charlie stared at it, the setting sun barely illuminating the rich red fruit bucket, her eyes fixed on the container.

Plopping down beside the bucket, Charlie pulled open the lid and picked up one of the berries, tossing it into her mouth and closing her eyes. She took another one, and then another one, until she'd made a dent in the container, its absence filling her mouth. She almost choked, unable to swallow.

Charlie opened her eyes, reaching down into the container again, and spotted a strawberry that still had its green stem. She picked it up, running her finger over the familiar, leafy texture. The odd man out.

Charlie began to chew the strawberries in her mouth, swallowed, and with an empty mouth and fingers stained red, began to cry.

THE SICKNESS

Lucas never liked visiting his grandmother's house.

If not for the suffocating heat of a log cabin without AC in the summer, the ruthless mosquitos, or the bland and nearly colorless food, he had to use her boxy, dial-up computer to feed his virtual pets.

Having to wait as the computer gradually displayed his pets on the screen made him feel The Sickness. Lucas would do *anything* not to feel The Sickness.

The computer was on the upper floor of the cabin. The "office" consisted of an extended section of floor space, built out just off the top of the stairs like an extendable arm, the front helm of the upstairs floor. The open room was surrounded by constructed model planes Lucas' grandfather had hung up when the cabin was first built, one of the many relics he'd left behind after his passing. The planes soared in their stationary flight paths just above the desk, and Lucas often found himself staring up at them as he waited for the computer to finish its song of whirls and beeps as it came to life.

Lucas loved his virtual pets, and he had all sorts of them. There was the snake, Ruby, a cat named Arthur, twin polar bears named Ice and Snow, and a beagle named Spike.

His animals made The Sickness disappear; the knotting in his stomach and cold, clammy sweat across his forehead gave way once he saw the smiling faces of his favorite pets. Not being able to care for his virtual animals made Lucas particularly nervous. He fretted about them over dinner with his parents and grandmother, anxiously awaiting the moment he could break away from them and bolt upstairs to boot up the computer.

At only eight, he thought it was pretty impressive that he could care for all of these animals by himself, a whole zoo's worth of creatures under his adoration. He fed them, made sure they all made their annual vet appointments, and bought them clothes and toys for each of their birthdays. Lucas never missed a single one.

Lucas loved these animals, and that's why he hated trips north to visit his grandmother. The computer never loaded his pets in the frame correctly, and it took hours for him to get through his daily routine of ensuring each one had been adequately attended to. His animals loaded pixel by pixel on the small screen, their expressions barely discernible as he gave them treats or their favorite toys. The reactions were always so delayed, the animals frozen and hesitant as Lucas slowly clicked and dragged the snacks from the menu toward the animal's half-visible mouth.

In the afternoons spent walking around historic monuments depicting early civilizations or by the coastline, Lucas hoped he hadn't missed his pets learning a new trick or finding buried treasure.

It wasn't that Lucas didn't want to spend time with his parents or his grandmother; he just had another responsibility. It weighed on him throughout the days spent away from the animals, no matter how much fun he knew he should be having. Lucas' pets were everything to him, and anxious thoughts of them getting sick or dying whispered into his ears with every hour he spent away from them. He couldn't escape it. It just had to be done, or The Sickness would come back.

This was the last night that Lucas and his parents were spending at his grandmother's cabin, and Lucas couldn't wait to get back home to feed his pets on his father's sleek, modern work laptop. It moved quickly, each of his pets popping up on the screen instantly, allowing Lucas to move through his routine three times faster than when he was at his grandmother's.

As his grandmother's computer whirled and looped, Lucas tapped his fingers impatiently on the desk, digging his fingernail into the wood until he'd left a mark. The waiting was only amplifying The Sickness, as it always did. The moments before Lucas logged into his pet portal were the worst part, where The Sickness grew most intense, and he felt he would fall out of the stiff wooden chair, paralyzed by it.

He heard his parents talking with his grandmother on the back deck, only the tops of their heads visible in the narrow window space he had from the desk. They bobbed along together as if synchronizing in some kind of dance as they conversed.

Lucas spotted his grandmother's short-cropped white hair, the stiffest of the floating heads at almost eighty-eight years old. She turned to look across the deck and then towards the lake the cabin butted up against. Lucas noticed the sun was setting, which he hadn't seen once the whole time they'd been there. The evenings were usually reserved for his pets.

His grandmother had asked him about his virtual animals only once, confused when his mother tried to explain why Lucas needed to use her ancient computer that usually sat collecting dust upstairs.

"He's got some pets that he needs to feed," his mother explained, as empathetic and gentle as possible.

"Pets?" his grandmother asked. "Where? What's he feeding them with?"

"They're online, mom," his mother continued. "Can you just let him use the computer?"

"I don't understand how he's got pets on that thing. Like in an email?"

"No, mom, not like that."

The computer stopped making whirring noises, and Lucas began clicking around to load the internet and get to his pets. In the new silence, he could hear the conversation between his parents and grandmother on the porch.

"He struggled a lot this year," his mom remarked, just barely audible to Lucas upstairs. His dad's voice was much less soft.

"His grades have been bad, and he's not making any friends," his dad continued. "Let's not sugarcoat it, Christy."

"He's just... shy. He's not like you, Ralph. Just because he's your son doesn't make him your mini-me."

Lucas' stomach got that funny feeling again, like when he couldn't feed his pets. He realized it was the same feeling he got in class, and his teacher called on him when he didn't know the answer because he couldn't see the board. It was the same feeling he had when he watched his old group of friends start hanging out at recess without him when he got kicked out of safety patrol because his grades slipped too low. The feeling always came right before The Sickness.

Besides the nice school counselor lady, he'd never told anyone about The Sickness because he was sure his mom would just take him to the doctor, and his dad would think he was just a wuss.

He had to deal with the Sickness on his own; he'd decided, puffing out his chest as he walked back from the counselor's office.

It was just the way it was.

Lucas was just happy his grandmother let him use the computer; he couldn't imagine having to go two weeks without caring for his pets. The thought made him feel sick in his stomach, his throat growing dry, and his forehead beaded with sweat as he thought about logging on and seeing that all his animals were dead.

The Sickness intensified, and he could feel the scary, shaky feeling rattling inside his head, the unyielding panic as if he would surely die that very moment. Lucas imagined himself pushing the thought away, like the nice counselor at school had told him to do once whenever he didn't like a thought he was having.

Push, push, PUSH!

Lucas closed his eyes, picturing himself behind an impossibly sized box, throwing his whole weight into the side until the thought slid entirely out of frame.

The computer screen gradually came to life with Ruby the snake, who flicked her tongue at a snail's pace and curled into the center of her virtual enclosure.

Lucas loved that Ruby was red like a gemstone or a strawberry on most of her body, but the back of her blended into a deep blue. Lucas had only seen snakes look like that on gummy worms that his mom would sometimes buy him from the gas station after a particularly rough day at school.

Ruby also had exactly thirty-two spots along her back. Lucas knew because he counted them over and over as she slithered back and forth before he gave her a snack. Counting Ruby's spots always made The Sickness go away, so even though he knew the answer, he did it anyway.

Twenty-seven, twenty-eight, twenty-nine, thirty, thirty-one—

Lucas felt The Sickness fading just as the upstairs of the cabin grew dark. He wiped the sweat from his palms on his blue shorts, leaving two symmetrical marks down the legs. The light from the computer screen illuminated the room, warm against Lucas' face, but it was not enough to keep the space from becoming a bit too dark. He frowned.

Lucas couldn't remember where the light switch was, so reaching out, he felt around the room, walking away from the computer screen.

He ran his hands along the wall, observing as the texture of the wood changed from smooth to coarse and back again before Lucas' fingers found a cool plastic light switch that he flicked on.

The room was fully illuminated, light bouncing off all corners of the elevated office space and open upstairs. The bulbs of the cabin were soft, old, and gave the space a distinct feeling of coziness. It was the opposite of Lucas's lighting in his bedroom at home and the big, cold lights of school classrooms. Those lights reminded him of hospitals or his dad's office, detached and unnerving, and they always made him feel The Sickness.

Turning away from the light switch, Lucas saw that some of the lights were hidden inside the floating paper plane models above the desk. The paper wings muffled some of the brighter tones of the light, yellowed paper turning the model planes into their own tiny stars.

He had never seen the planes like this before, lit up enough to see all of the details cut into their wings and across the tails.

The Sickness continued to fade from his stomach, and Lucas plopped down on the aged blue carpet away from the computer and looked up at the different planes; his eyes darting from left to right and back again.

He studied the new details he could identify on each of the planes; the way some had small silver details on each of the wheels, the folded and fanned paper tails on others now emphasized in cast shadows and shapes from each tiny, glowing light.

There were fifteen planes in total. Lucas tallied through each of them three times, ensuring he studied each one before moving on to the next one, the same attention he gave to his pets. He counted their stripes, admired the creases in their wheels, and how broad their wings were.

The planes moved slightly from the breeze of the open windows to circulate the summer air. Lucas grinned at even their smallest animations as if each was intentional and not at the whim of the gentle wind from outside, like Ruby's slow slithering across his computer screen.

It made him feel safe.

Ruby, Lucas thought and started to stand up to run back to the computer, but for the first time, he didn't feel compelled to. He wasn't trying to fight The Sickness anymore; it had faded entirely as soon as he'd started looking up at the planes. For some unknown reason, he knew that maybe, going a day without seeing the animals, they'd probably be okay.

Before he knew it, Lucas' eyes grew heavy as he watched the planes rock slowly back and forth underneath the warm light, voyaging in place. Maybe, he would journey along with them, like a brave fighter pilot or a superhero, unafraid and free of The Sickness forever.

Lucas fell asleep on the carpet, where his mother would later find him and move him to the bed. She would kiss his forehead before walking across to the office, where she'd turn off the computer just before she hit the light.

COMMERCIAL SPACE

"And if you look to the right here," the tour guide cooed eagerly into the microphone, as if revealing a secret, "you'll find the remnants of the last county clerk's office in the city."

The busy tour bus "*oohed*" and "*ahhed*," pressing their holographic cameras out of the open windows towards the disheveled bricks in the shape of what remained of the previous foundation. The only thing that remained on the site of the ruins, near where you could assume would have once been the entryway, was a newly mounted golden plaque with an open book.

"This is an exceptional spot, folks," the tour guide grinned, exposing his modified teeth, carved to look like they belonged inside an animal's mouth.

"This was one of the last information resources about early settlers, agricultural production, and prehistoric communication, such as text messages, email, and even letter writing."

The bus responded in a flurry of additional photos,

pressing the center of their palms to upload their experience to the centralized cloud, much to the envy of friends who couldn't afford the journey here or had their Visa denied before their teleportation departure date.

Many families couldn't believe this country even had access to much of the modern technology only available across the wealthier and less war-torn countries. It was unexpected that this place would have access to modern innovation after decades of warlord rule, imperial control, and re-colonization. Most of the travelers on the bus had made sure to get additional immunization and came with an armed guard before booking their tickets to come here.

Globally, most foreigners had depicted this place as increasingly dangerous and occupied by an authoritarian state, so many were surprised to find much of anything left in the landscapes.

This mystery made it one of the most popular places in the world to travel to. People had a rampant curiosity about what it would look like here, the desire to brag to friends and family that they'd *really* been to this place, not just in virtual reality. They'd met with actual people and shared their experiences as open-minded global citizens.

Besides, a certain level of exclusivity came with being able to travel here. You had to be healthy enough to mitigate the radiation exposure and rich enough to afford the teleportation fee in and out of the country.

Only the elite could afford to see such a poor place.

"We'll stop here for a few minutes, folks," the tour guide called up front. "Feel free to look around the monument, and then we'll pack up for lunch at an approved restaurant by the State Bureau of Tourist Guidance."

Several tourists opened their private doors in and out of the large bus and stepped out towards the remains, not before pulling on their masks and skin protectors while ensuring their required cross necklaces were visible on the top of their clothes. The air outside was thick and heavy, chemicals and oxygen made warm by the heat of the modern North

American summer at 122 degrees.

"It's a shame they haven't been able to redevelop this area," one of the tourists remarked, digging the toe of her shoe into the lifeless soil. "I read once that there were thousands of different species here. Better yet, this was a huge city, with stunning skyscrapers before any of the rest of the world had built anything half as tall."

The other tourists nodded, barely listening as they made their way around the sparse remains of the perimeter, one of the men catching the front of their shoe on a small gold plaque buried in the sand. On top was an incredibly faint "M." He kept walking.

Plants had become few and far between in this region, though it had once been rich with crops and forestry of all kinds, providing for much of the country and the world. After the country collapsed, it provided for the winning nations that it had failed to defend itself from. After the failure of the first revolutionary leader, it provided for another.

And so on.

"I hear that once China finishes on Mars, they're coming back to do something here," one man said, pointing down toward the ground.

"All this land is just perfect for increased production space."

"I don't know," the woman replied, pulling on the cross around her neck. "Weren't there people that lived here? Where are they now?"

The man shrugged.

"They're not here anymore."

The woman dug her heel back into the dirt, studying the hole left behind as she twisted her ankle. The soil separated into two small hills around the outside of her shoe, soon blown away by a passing wind.

The building could have been immense, multi-story even, though no information was available to prove it. Besides the plaque with the photo of the book or the discarded "M" in the dirt, the site had no information about what it had been used for, who had built it, and who had destroyed it. Everything only indicated that it had, at one time, existed.

"Take my picture!" a little girl called to her father, tugging on the charging cord of his oxygen mask and pulling him towards the small golden book plaque.

"Okay, okay, I'll take your picture." The father reached into his pocket and pulled out his holographic camera, holding one finger against his brain to record into the cloud.

"Smile, Pandora."

Underneath her oxygen mask, Pandora's lips turned upwards into a grin, and as she leaned in toward the sign, you could just make out the upturned corners of her mouth.

"Come on, everyone!" the tour guide called from outside the bus. "Time to head out."

Single-file families began their marches back and away from the remains, Pandora scurrying behind her dad, the last to board.

She turned back one last time to look at the empty space, her oxygen mask growing itchy on her face. She wished she didn't have to wear it, but her dad told her there was no good air left here to breathe.

Her father picked her up and returned to their seats, waiting for the bus door to close before reaching over and pulling off her oxygen mask.

Staring out the window, Pandora traced her finger over the window along the outline of the building, and just as the bus pulled forward, she closed her eyes, imagining the real thing.

SECOND BEDROOM

Their new place smelled like cigarettes and seafood, no larger than a shoebox and in the oldest part of the city.

There was no modern downtown coffee shop or far-future-themed escape room with immersion elements like oxygen masks and real dirt. It was an unimpressive neighborhood of clustered people that called the place home.

Celeste found a spot for the last of Brandon's mother's silverware she'd donated to the two of them, the final bin in the last box. They were officially moved in, and now this place was their home too.

Pasta was boiling on the stove, a tail of steam reaching up and curling at the end towards the low-hanging ceiling. The space was the nicest that the two of them could afford, close enough to Brandon's work that he didn't increase their Net-Carbon Index too much by driving too far, slightly larger than some of the micro-apartments closer to the downtown.

The best part of their new place was that it had a second bedroom.

Currently, their mattress was on the floor of the larger bedroom, shoved in the corner with unmade sheets and blankets tangled on the top. Brandon had been at work for the better part of the day, and Celeste wanted to make sure he came home to something that felt remotely more like they *lived* there than when they moved in earlier in the week.

The timer on Celeste's phone called out. The pasta had finished cooking. Celeste drained the pot and let the pasta rest in the sauce she'd been casually stirring while swooping between piles looking for two bowls.

Brandon had set up their TV just this morning, an older model that still required an active outlet, and it buzzed the evening news in a dull whisper that matched the uncomfortably cool fluorescent lights. Celeste reminded herself to ask the landlord if they could change the lights to something less sterile and schoollike as she divided the pasta up. Brandon would be home any minute.

Alarmed by the clutter, hungry, and tired, Celeste grabbed a bowl of pasta for herself and crept around the piles scattered throughout the room and towards the smaller second bedroom near the back of the apartment.

Small was probably an exaggeration when describing the space, as the room was barely larger than Celeste's parent's pantry had been, with a small window that looked out the back alley behind their building. It was as if it had been a last-minute decision by the builder and probably should have just been part of the main bedroom behind the other side of the wall.

The pasta was too hot to eat, so Celeste stirred it around before placing it beside her feet on the faded carpet and sat down. The space was surprisingly welcoming, with blank walls and nothing crowding the different corners of the room. The last of the daylight was slipping down below the windowsill, the noisy bustling of the city just audible in the distance.

It didn't feel like home here yet, even with all of the time Celeste had spent trying to get it ready. She chalked it up to how new it all was and how many things had changed in such a short amount of time. Nothing was familiar yet, and that was what made places feel like home.

Celeste wondered what she and Brandon would do with this second bedroom. She had many ideas, mapped in hidden notes and tabs on her phone. Maybe the two of them could share a work-from-home office, or perhaps it could be a guest bedroom for her parents when they came from overseas to visit. There was always making it into a hangout space, considering their current living room was lackluster at best.

Or...

Celeste slid her phone out of her back pocket, navigating through grocery lists and house fixes to her private notes and the one labeled "*The Second Bedroom.*"

Beneath photos of lush orange couches and articles about maximizing in a minimal space, Celeste spotted the light green baby room she'd been eyeing for the last year. The walls were painted a rich mossy green, the carpet a plush beige. Across one of the walls was a crib, accented with gold details, just below a miniature animal mural on the wall.

Celeste clicked on the photos and zoomed in to look at her favorite part of the room; the ceiling freckled with small stars.

She had dreamed about having them in her room as a kid, envious of her friends who did. When she'd sleep over at their houses, she'd stare up at them for hours, encapsulated by the world created inside the four walls. It was as if she could imagine herself being anywhere in the world that she wanted.

When Celeste first discovered the photo, she hadn't thought anything of it. It's not even like she wanted a kid, but the idea of the space just made her heart feel warm in a way that she couldn't explain.

Celeste found herself daydreaming about dates and names for babies she knew she'd never have, like *Sage* or *Pandora*, two of which she liked. She imagined picking them up from school, buying them an afternoon snack, watching them get older, every vision as vivid as her real life.

The daydream about creating the nursery felt better than her short stint on Tenophin, a depression medication she'd seen on TV and asked her doctor about that made her feel entirely disconnected from reality. The nursery was like a warm blanket, a cool and quiet room, creating calmness within her body without relying on a chemical to do so. The picture had saved Celeste from several anxiety attacks, but she knew she had to break her dependence on it.

Brandon and Celeste knew they didn't have the Net Carbon Index capacity to have a child. She'd combed the reports for years; the average recommended salary for a family of three had shot through the ceiling. Besides, paying to send a child to elementary, middle, and high school, and if they were lucky, a two-year college program, was out of the question.

Celeste knew they didn't have the money, resources, or guarantee of a future to offer to a child; she knew that as well as anything. Still, she'd not been able to shake her mind from the photo of the green nursery, hiding it at the bottom of her notes and returning to it only when she knew she was alone.

Celeste hadn't ever had an unending desire to be a parent. She loved her career, her freedom, her friends, and the love she and Brandon had now. She knew what having a baby meant, what it would require both of them to give up. But the idea of bringing another person into their lives wasn't something that scared her as much as she always thought it would, which in turn, made her guilt over the green baby room photo even harder to bear.

Sprawling down onto her back, Celeste extended her arms and felt the carpet brush against every inch of her exposed skin. The ceiling was still an empty, pale white, but if Celeste closed her eyes tight enough and pulled in her chest to hold her breath, she could almost see it, stars like freckles across the nose of the second bedroom's face.

The front door rattled and opened, the sound of a key turning into the lock radiating through the apartment.

"Celeste?"

"In here!" she called across the house.

"You will not believe the story my mom told me about her

old friend Cleo—"

Celeste heard Brandon drop his stuff on the counter and step through the apartment until he peered around the corner to where she was lying. He grinned, pausing.

"Tired?"

"Only a little," Celeste replied, sitting up and reaching for her phone to close the note tab with the baby room pictures. "I made pasta, it's on the counter if you want some."

"Exceptional." Brandon grinned. "The apartment looks great. It seems like everything's unpacked."

Celeste slid her phone back into her pocket. "Just a matter of putting it all away." She hesitated. "And, setting up this room."

Brandon stepped into the second bedroom, his work shoes leaving deep impressions on the carpet as he walked to stand by the window. She wanted to tell him to remove his shoes, but the words stuck in her head. Specks of dirt from his commute through the city found their way across the floor.

"There is a lot we could do here." Brandon nodded, looking up at the walls and back down to the carpet. "It's small, but it's some good space."

Watching him pace, Celeste curled her fingers around her phone she'd stowed away in her pocket, the tips of her fingers warm against the machine, daring her to pull it out again. She felt her palms start to sweat, her heart thumping.

Pressing his fingers against the glass until it left small streaks of warmth, Brandon grinned.

"It would be nice to have a home office."

Celeste swallowed. "You think?"

Brandon stepped away from the window, looking up at each empty wall, his eyes soaking in the free space like a canvas.

"I've wanted to have a place where I can go if I need to bring work home. Keep the tax documents. Put the extra TV."

Celeste nodded in agreement, her heart dropping to her stomach, pushing a smile up her lips.

"Besides," Brandon said, walking up behind Celeste,

wrapping his long arms around her shoulders, cocooning her. "I think it's kind of nice to imagine you working here. Painting. Something creative, maybe?"

He leaned his head down and kissed the top of her head, brushing his hand through the back of her hair. "Sounds like a dream to me. What do you think?"

Celeste rubbed her fingertips along the top of her phone. Brandon's cologne was all over her shirt, and she could feel his pulse through her back and against her shoulder where he rested his neck. Her hand lingered on her phone in her back pocket, the warm buzz, the ceiling stars.

What good would it do?

Turning herself around in his arms, Celeste looked up at him.

"I think it's a great idea."

YELLOW LINE

In the back of the bus, Augustus realized he needed to drop out of college. It wasn't a decision he'd taken lightly, instead, riding for hours on the Yellow Bus Route to think about whether or not he was really sure of it.

Augustus sorted through his half-read textbooks and incoherent notes, skimming his journal for traces of life or vibrance and finding none of the sorts. Beady-eyed older men stared back at him from the faded pages of the textbook, written in the 80s and serving as an educational time capsule of sorts.

What do any of you know anyway? Augustus thought, skimming a page with several men with slick-combed hair in fitted suits. Their stoic expressions felt hollow, empty, and devoid of any emotion, even though they were smiling.

Augustus had never thought he was meant to work in marketing, but it was an easy choice when he finished his general education credits to tell his academic advisor that he liked being creative and writing. He asked her about the creative writing program or the music program, but she'd steered him in a different direction.

"Marketing!" She grinned, fawning out a series of papers and pamphlets across her dark wooden desk. "It's the perfect place for people who *want* to be creative but also need a day job. You can create *all* kinds of stuff, graphics, blog posts, sales enablement messaging. It's the *perfect* place for someone like you, Augustus."

Someone like you, meaning *someone that was otherwise unskilled and bad at math and science but could kind of create and needed to be a functioning force in the economy.*

He didn't blame her; what else could she encourage him to do? Play the lottery scratchers his whole life and hope for the best?

His academic advisor slid the papers across the desk and into his hands, where he held them through the rest of the meeting and for the entirety of the walk back to his parent's house, where he'd moved back after running out of money to afford his apartment. His fingers had left deep imprints on each of the pages.

He'd never forget the look on his mother's face, hands gracefully folded around the sides of the casserole dish as she pulled it from the oven.

"Marketing," she grinned. "That's a great career path, Gus. You could work for anybody!"

His father had echoed the enthusiasm, though half-heartedly. He'd imagined Gus as a lawyer, politician, or future CEO. "As long as you go to work for a *real* company," he shrugged, slicing into his lasagna and taking a bite. "None of that startup nonsense. You wanna be in one of those big buildings downtown, don't you?"

"We'd be happy wherever you go," his mother smiled. "Your *career* should make you happy, don't forget that."

Augustus remembered the lasagna being overcooked that night and not believing what his mother was saying, but wanting to try in the same way he politely swallowed the mushy noodles. He sat through his marketing classes, taking notes on audience insights, the power of language to convince people to change their minds without directly selling to them, and graphic design classes, where he was reprimanded for too much experimentation in his ad mock-ups. Still, he pushed, but the further he went, the further he fell away from the plan he'd wanted to be on.

Marketing wasn't all that creative, he'd realized, and folded his notebook over, closed.

The bus jerked over a speed bump, knocking Augustus' pen back into the seat. He fumbled around, looking for it.

Marketing involved lots of recycling other people's garbage, relying on half-truths and ego to convince people to spend money. Marketing was creating problems and offering immediate solutions for things your organization happened to be perpetuating. Was he supposed to conflate creativity with spinning someone else's false narrative?

Augustus wanted to tell real stories, like the ones he'd read or heard in music since he was a kid. He wanted to tell stories that got people in touch with themselves and reality and didn't force them to a singular conclusion of consuming a product or a service. He wanted to write characters, not personas for a whitepaper. He wanted to draw again without giving up on pieces because he'd spent all his energy on making something for someone else in blocky, corporate-approved text.

This couldn't possibly be what his life was destined to be, telling someone else's story.

So, after another afternoon class spent reformatting a piece he'd been surprisingly proud of to fit into a bland corporate animation mock-up, he realized he needed to figure something else out.

He would not do this a day longer. He couldn't. It made his chest hurt and confined him to doing nothing while the world caught fire in a collapsing economic system. He didn't want to watch tragedies unfold and ignore them because he had a deadline for an ad about cranberry juice due at midnight.

He couldn't do it.

He just couldn't do it.

Grabbing his pen from the bus chair, Augustus began to sketch a half oval before it evolved into the partially obscured side of a distant hill, discerning the borders between the hill and the horizon by shading with the pen. The blue hill cut across a paling sky, a distant sun making its descent behind.

Augustus liked riding the bus because it was the only place he could think. Between classes and his parent's bickering, he felt he hadn't had a moment to ask himself what he wanted in years, only drifting between the idea of independence or alternative realities where he was an actualized version of himself.

"Marketing is a career they can't automate," his mother read from her tablet at the dinner table. "See, you'll have job security as the robot population increases."

Her grin was shaky; she wanted so badly to believe that Augustus would be safe as a marketer. That he wouldn't have to fall back on them again. That he wouldn't get hurt. His mother had built up the idea of security like an impenetrable nest, made of solid steel, unwavering as if she could preserve him in amber if his career was something failure-proof. Something without risk.

His parents were raised in a world where your career did keep you safe, where your job was an undeniable net that kept you from ever hitting the ground.

His father had spent a career working in a credit card company's towering office downtown, the bottom floor now a sleek robot-run coffee shop. His mother was a paralegal. Their lives had found stability in the confines of careers that were streamlined, but the world had changed. The nets weren't real anymore, no matter what you did.

Augustus could fail at being a marketer and end up on the street the same way he could fail at being an artist and end up on the street. He could get sick sitting in his desk chair for eight hours every day, the same way he could get sick writing the next great American novel.

Hell, he'd seen the news just a couple of weeks ago about

the recent college graduate who'd been killed in a car accident. Another person who did everything right, according to the broadcast, and still ended up with the short end of the stick.

The way Augustus saw it, he could die giving a presentation on his KPIs or at a reading of his first published book.

And he knew which thought he liked better.

The bus popped over another speed bump, sending Augustus' pen carving straight through the drawn skyline he'd carved across the college-ruled paper. Frowning, he brought the pen back towards him, adding small ruffles around the top of the line, watching as it transformed into a tree, just as disruptive but more appropriate.

"Excuse me," the bus driver called up front, knocking on the separation glass that isolated her from the passengers on the bus. Augustus looked up.

"This is our last stop. I need to empty the bus."

"Oh-" Augustus stammered, folding his notebooks closed and placing his books into his bag.

He hadn't expected to be arriving at the stop this quickly. What was he going to tell his parents when he saw them? He didn't have a plan yet. He didn't know anything about what he wanted to be doing or where he wanted to be. For the first time in a long time, he felt he knew what he liked and didn't like.

Maybe that was all there was to it.

Augustus walked up to the front of the bus and scanned his student ID for the last time, jumping off the bus and into the patch of dead grass that had welcomed him to his parent's street for as long as he could remember.

Looking out in the distance, he spotted a familiar hillside and setting sun, the last of the light waning in shades of pink, orange, and red, shaded almost identically to the mirror image he was holding in his closed blue notebook.

In this distance, three lines of birds crossed over the street, their wings flapping as they ventured west, chasing the last of the light. Augustus watched as they swooped together beyond the extending arm of sunlight sinking into the hillside.

These birds always flew along this bus route, and he'd known that forever, swooping up and over the hill until they landed at the base of a cliff by the lake.

Opening his notebook, Augustus made a note to add the birds to the drawing later. He let himself memorize every swoop, perhaps, something worth replicating.

THE FEMUR

It happened at night.

He'd not brought anything with him besides a large rock he'd found near the entrance of the cave where his family lived. He was determined to find an animal to skin, to collect another layer of fur to get the tribe through the cold season. They had all begun to grow so skinny; the little ones had jagged bones poking through the narrow parts of their flesh, the elders sacrificing the last of their layers to huddle the youngest together in insulated groups whenever they managed to get a fire going.

He'd thought about them huddled together in the back of the cave, the moisture dripping down in steady drops against the top of their heads, making them shiver. There were no other spaces nearby to move to; he'd checked for that first, only encountering several large animals with the same idea huddled under thick trees or at the bottom of rock formations. He often found dark red berries in these spots, biting into the flesh and letting the sweet fruit fill his mouth before he slipped back toward the tribe.

This was the third time he'd gone out at night. Most of the time, no one in the tribe dared to leave the cave before the sun had risen, expanding over the top of the valley and filling even the densest forests with light.

Many elders believed that evil spirits existed in the dark, vicious manifestations of gods and monsters, greedy and demanding sacrifice to ensure survival. They would trick you into believing they were a kindred spirit, offering wisdom or guidance, only to lure you into deep bodies of water or off the edges of cliffs to your death.

He had started going out not to face the spirits but to attempt survival. The daylight hours were not enough time to ensure that enough food was being collected for everybody. They needed more time, time he believed they were not going to get otherwise.

He believed, perhaps, the spirits would take pity on him for trying.

Now, he looked down at his body, his right leg split at an unnatural angle at the top of his thigh, stranded at the bottom of a hill of dense brush and trees, and realized perhaps the tribe had been right.

He hadn't seen the large tree root at the top of the hill, rising from the dirt and uncurling like a snake across the path he'd walked so many times before. Losing his balance, he'd tripped over the top of it, catching his balance too late as intense pain and then numbness spread through the top of his leg.

He'd seen this happen to animals before, their limbs sprawled out and unusable before them, dragging their bodies through the dirt until they couldn't move any further. He believed trees were the only living thing that could lose an extremity and continue to exist. For everything else, if you lost the ability to move forward, you were done for.

He rolled slowly onto his left hip, the burning and discomfort in his right side beginning to spread. He'd never been in pain like this before, even with previous falls and broken teeth. This was a loss of his mobility, the living distinction between animals and plants: the ability to roam.

He looked up towards the top of the hill, feeling the wind as it swam through the branches of the trees. He'd always liked the wind, the way it moved the same way the water did, only invisible. Though he'd never told the rest of the tribe, he believed that the wind was a messenger from the future, and if they could understand it, they would know the world's fate.

He wasn't sure what that meant or even how to start translating for the wind. He'd tried, but the only messages he'd receive from the wind were frightening or dangerous. He'd see a future made dark, a dark sky, dark soil, and faces made expressionless. He'd seen a world without the tribe.

Sometimes, the wind would send him visions in his sleep of a world held within walls. People lived in caves reaching into the sky, narrow and sharp as the fingers of a god. His hands had turned a distinctive shade of red as if he'd killed an animal. He would find himself standing in the middle of these massive, sky-bound caves, alarmed by the noise echoing between them.

His heart pounded like he was being chased, though when he looked back, not a single person or animal was behind him; he was alone. He hated that feeling, the pressing weight against his chest he felt when he couldn't name the threat he was faced with—the invisible enemy, somehow far more distinct than anything he could see.

The vision finished as he ran out towards a distant body of water. He recognized it as the lake they drank from, the only place that remained familiar throughout the rest of the frightening vision. Once clear, the water turned a dark shade of brown when he reached for it. No matter how hard he washed, the dirt and dust on his hands never came off until, eventually, all the water dried up.

These dreams frightened him, but he couldn't tell anyone about them. What good would it do if he told them the wind believed that the world they knew would no longer exist someday?

What would they live for?

The wind blew several leaves across the top of his face, one landing in his tangled mess of hair. It was a brilliant shade of red, dark and deep as his stained fingers in the vision. He pulled it from his hair and ran his finger along the edge, feeling the ruffled texture against his skin.

He closed his eyes, took a deep breath, and sank into the dirt. The elders had taught them all about how to prepare for death, it required an acceptance that this was how things were and there was nothing else that could be done to change it. Whenever an elder prepared for death, they often disappeared for long hours into the forest, returning with new canyons carved between their brows, bearing the kind of knowledge you're only gifted right before the end.

There is a special kind of silence in the forest, one he'd always loved dearly. If this was where he would return to the soil, perhaps, there were worse places to die. Maybe in the lake. Or in the world that plagued his nightmares. He'd never want to die in a place like that.

The wind spread across the top of his covered chest, and he pulled open the front of his covering, letting it leave bumps on his chest as he shivered.

He let the fear drift out of his body, and travel deep into the ground and away from him. He sent it away, he would not carry his grief into death. He would bring only his spirit, vowing to protect the forest for as long as it stood.

If this was the sacrifice the spirits asked for, this is what he'd give them.

If this was what kept the rest of the tribe alive, this is what had to be done.

The wind rippled over him, grazing fingers over his eyelashes before everything finally stood still.

Peace.

Nothing.

He heard the trees swaying gently, the rustling of the leaves tickling his ears, though he didn't open his eyes to see it. He observed, blind, let the leaves fill his consciousness. The ache in his leg began to fade, the dirt growing warm across his exposed skin like a fur blanket.

Maybe this was the place he'd been looking for.

Suddenly, a red light glowed through his closed eyes. He clenched them closed tighter, trying to block any light from entering.

He had accepted death. What was asking him to defy it?

Was it the spirits?

Was it the wind?

Slowly, he let his eyes flutter open and realized that the sun was coming up. Through the trees to the forest floor, he could see the light beginning to shift through the branches, its streaming fingers reaching entirely through the canopy and down into the dirt beside him, his leg growing warm.

The others would be getting up soon.

Maybe this wasn't death.

He took another deep breath, swallowed, opened his mouth, and called out for the first time. He called out again, louder this time, and he heard the sound bounce between the trees and up the hill to the cave. Taking one more deep breath, he called out as loud as he could before he slumped backward and braced himself against a tree.

The wind was the first to reply and dropped another leaf on the top of his face. He didn't remove it; instead, he let it rest on his cheek, tickling against the bottom of his nose.

"Ah!"

A voice grunted from the top of the hill.

"Ah!" He returned.

"Ah!" "Ah!" "Ah!"

Several voices shouted from the top of the hill, the forest filling with the sound. He hears several feet running down the side of the hill, nearing closer and closer to him until he is face to face with several members of the tribe. Their eyes scattered across his body, but then landed on his leg.

No one moved. Each of them looked between each other and back to him, studying the alarming angle of his leg against the ground. He looks each of them over, studying their jagged bones, the hollow parts of their faces, bruised and broken fingernails, and matted hair.

He'd watched so many of them grow up, helped raise their children, shared in their fear, shared in their joy. He'd shared in their lives.

He remembered a moment in the spring when a group of them had gone off to hunt, bringing back several large birds and smaller mammals, enough to feed the whole tribe for several weeks. They'd gathered together around the fire, sharing the meal, looking out from the mouth of the cave into the vast and expansive habitat that was theirs. They told stories about their visions of the future, danced, and left markings in the cave for spiritual protection to share with the babies once they were older. They gathered, they slept, and they lived, together.

This was his family.

People he knew, and the people he'd done everything to protect.

A woman stepped forward, pulling off part of the bottom of her cover, her exposed skin pricked against the cold wind. She knelt beside him and ran her fingers against the outside of his leg. He struggled not to wince as she wrapped the bottom of the fur underneath his leg, moving the bone back into place. She tightened the fur, knelt her head down, and gently placed her hand against him.

A bird called out from above, and then several more, forming a sharp 'V' shape as they soared higher, the wind pulling their wings forward.

Wordlessly, members of the tribe surrounded him, locked arms underneath him, and lifted him off the ground. He shouted out in pain, but his leg did not move. Several others held his leg straight, and the others still held him up behind his shoulders as they all walked up the hill.

His face grew warm underneath the light, and though his eyes burned, he continued to look up towards the sky and watched the birds.

They inched closer to the top of the hill, their journey in lockstep with the sun as it climbed up and over the top of the forest.

As the light rose, he looked down at the root he'd tripped over and realized in the light it was only a branch, broken off the side of a tree and discarded at the bottom. It was smaller than he'd perceived it, and as the group neared its side, one member of the tribe knelt down and moved it off of the path and slid it down to the bottom of the hill and out of sight.

The group rounded out of the forest and neared the cave entrance, where several other members of the tribe gathered around a fire someone had started. They left him beside the fire, set him down so that his leg remained straight out before him, and stepped back.

His face felt wet. Raindrops pooled in his eyes and rolled down the top of his cheek.

He looked out into the distance, beyond the tribe, beyond the side of the hill, and out towards the lake. He admired its depth, the way it caught the sunlight off the water and directed it back towards them. The small waves bounced between the different sides of the shore as they carried the wind, making it visible.

His leg ached, but for the first time, the wind promised him it would be okay.

POST CREDITS

Robin wondered if his life had reached an undeniable epilogue.

In the house he bought in his late thirties, the interior well-kept but now vintage compared to any modern achievements, he wondered if this was all that was left.

He'd lived in the same area since he was twenty-two years old. He and Maria, his wife who had passed away, never had children, so after she was gone, Robin spent the rest of his retirement between his front porch and the kitchen, drinking coffee and reading the newspaper.

Robin's neighbors were interesting.

He lived directly between a couple from England with two small children and a married couple who just happened to be WWE wrestlers. Both couples were exceptionally kind, trading off which of them would bring him food for the first few months after Maria died. They'd spend a few hours with him, ask him about Maria and what she was like, share small details about the days they'd had out in a world Robin was no longer part of, and then, they'd retreat to their private habitats and leave him alone.

Robin was left with his sweet but equally frustrating cat, Darby, who occasionally broke into the pantry to eat from his stash of candy. Sometimes he'd watch the dogwalker for the Pastor's dogs get pulled down the street by the two unrelenting dogs even Maria couldn't put up with. Robin hoped the girl's arm was healing alright.

Maybe Robin was ignorant about getting older. He had thought the loneliness his parents and grandparents had told him about was just something to chalk up as an old wive's tale or something that bitter adults said when they wanted to guilt their families into visiting.

None of it seemed like a fair or honest portrayal of what it was like to get old. They were being overdramatic and ungrateful even with the time they did get to spend with others. About all the time they'd *already* spent in the world.

However, at seventy-six, Robin believed that his grandmother *had* been as isolated as she'd said when he called her on his winter break from college or after he and his parents left her house after summer break because right now, he couldn't remember a time in his life when he'd been lonelier.

Still, he felt like he was being negative. Robin was in no way disappointed with the life that he'd lived. He was fulfilled by it. He'd lived the way he'd wanted to, and through every facet that had been difficult, he hadn't turned away or tuned out just to get through it.

He'd watched the city spring out from a small cluster of skyscrapers into soaring, mountain-high buildings. He'd seen the invention of the cell phone and the internet and watched as his wife lived ten years longer than the doctor initially said she would, thanks to modern medicine. He'd made lifelong friends, eaten incredible meals, and witnessed some of the most profound art he'd ever seen.

Robin had written a best-selling book, flown out to New York and Los Angeles for book signings and meetings with people who loved what he'd written, and told him that his words had changed their lives.

The months he'd spent writing were hard, on both him and Maria. He'd close his doors for weeks at a time, the two connecting only for brief meals and to say goodnight.

Yet, it had been worth it, every moment leading up to a release that was well received, recognized, and celebrated.

"When you lock yourself away for a little while," Maria had grinned, rubbing his shoulders and whispering to him before he sank back into his office, "you always come back with something that changes the world. That makes it all worth it to me."

And so, the two of them did make it worth it. They made the sacrifice worth it.

Maria and Robin spent many weekends volunteering at their local community center and spending time with children of all ages and backgrounds. They led projects that promoted reforestation in countries leveled by the rising heat waves, Maria taught their neighbors how to live off the land and dodge the rising cost of grocery store food. Maria ran for local office and won, championing greener transportation initiatives in the city and increasing access to public services.

The two of them threw parties and fostered deep and meaningful friendships. They celebrated community victories and relished the past and present with equal appreciation.

Robin didn't know too many people that had been able to do the things he had, and maybe that was making him feel guilty about feeling lonely.

Wasn't this what you were supposed to do?

Achieve all the things you wanted and then let yourself just bask in them for the rest of your life?

He supposed that's why this part felt like the epilogue.

Because it was true.

Robin had done everything he wanted; now, he was living in the aftermath, which was the phase no one ever seemed to talk about:

What came *after* happiness?

From the couch in his living room, Robin could see the different families across the street, one had a quiet teenage daughter, and another belonged to a middle-aged couple with adult children. The third one down had all of its lights off, the family of three with a small young boy visiting family, followed by the Pastor's family with their unruly dogs. Just down the road, a gas station, a drying lake, a new hotel, and a homeless encampment.

This was Robin's ecosystem, every person living their own distinct lives among his, as they did before him and as they would in some far future that he wouldn't live to see. They converged for short moments in their lives, and often, they never would again.

Robin stood up, brushed off his pants, and walked to the kitchen. He discarded his coffee mug and the morning paper, leaving them by the empty box of bandaids.

Opening his pantry, he moved the bread and peanut butter aside, and discarded to torn plastic remnants of Darby's candy stealing to reveal a chocolate croissant he'd bought for himself earlier in the week but forgotten about. He'd been doing this for a while now, buying the pastry on Monday when he visited the grocery store and tucking it away until he'd find it again and was able to treat it like a surprise rather than an expectation.

He pulled the croissant from its paper bag and bit into it, savoring the sweetness filling his mouth.

Robin looked out the window momentarily, watching the flickering of the inconsistent streetlights just beginning to come on, and tallied how many times they blinked.

Thirty-two.

He'd always had a thing for numbers.

Though the street was otherwise quiet, Robin heard the distinctive sound of traffic from the end of the rush hour commute, cars streaming down the road, and a honking bus.

In their garden, the last raised bed Maria planted before she passed was full of tomatoes, strawberries, basil, and carrots. When she got sick, she wanted to ensure he was never without the fresh vegetables they'd always grown together.

"If you take care of your garden, good things will grow

around it," Maria had promised as the pair filled the bed with soil. "Just like people."

Even as the heat intensified and the rain fell less frequently, Robin had made sure that Maria's plants were cared for. Change did not have to signal the end, only the opportunity to adapt.

Later, he'd go out and harvest the fresh fruits and vegetables, offering up the extras to his neighbors, but for now, he returned to the sofa to finish his croissant.

ABOUT THE AUTHOR

Vanessa Frances is the author of three poetry collections, written through her teenage and young adult life. She holds a BA in Digital Journalism and Media from Pennsylvania State University and is pursuing an MS in Environmental Law from Vermont Law and Graduate School. She works as a marketer, managing editor, musician, and dog walker.

Through Neighboring Windows is her first full-length collection.

VISIT VANESSA FRANCES ONLINE
@faaemusic on Instagram